16ᵗʰ-Century Feathers

In 1500 barely anyone in Europe wore feathers, yet 100 years later, they had become the height of fashion. Feather working was now a whole new trade and people were making a living simply from decorating feathers for clothes. This new fashion trend was inextricably linked to the Age of Discovery and the fact that European colonists were coming across exotic birds on their travels to the Americas. The ruling elites started to use them to signify their power and reach and feathers soon represented a sign of culture to Europeans. For Native Americans, feathers were never a fashion accessory but had always symbolized their communication with the spirit world and expressed celestial wisdom. Feathers fall from the sky and so on the other side of the Atlantic, they represented ascension in spiritual evolution to a higher plane.

I Am a Feather

BY LORNA DICKINSON

DORRANCE
PUBLISHING CO
EST. 1920
PITTSBURGH, PENNSYLVANIA 15238

Dorrance Publishing Co
585 Alpha Drive
Suite 103
Pittsburgh, PA 15238
Visit our website at *www.dorrancebookstore.com*

ISBN: 978-1-6495-7088-8
eISBN: 978-1-6495-7601-9

To my family,

Mike, Marshall and George,

for supporting my efforts

to prove that, alongside the wars and revolutions

that hog the headlines,

it was the warmth of a friendship

bridging two different cultures

that changed the course of history

over the last 400 years

and to

Jessie Little Doe Baird

for being the friendly voice across the Atlantic

that bridged the gaps in my story.

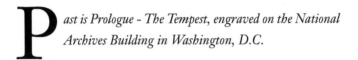

I AM A FEATHER

Past is Prologue - The Tempest, engraved on the National Archives Building in Washington, D.C.

Loved not wisely but too well – Othello

You taught me language, and my profit on't, Is, I know how to curse - The Tempest

More sinned against than sinning - King Lear

O brave new world that has such people in't - The Tempest

Unlucky deeds – like the base Indian, threw a pearl away, richer than all his tribe – Othello

That it should come to this? – Hamlet

Heat not a furnace for your foe so hot that it do singe yourself

Prologue

Dear Taylor,

A year is such a long time to be away from home.

Eleven hours from London and sixteen hours from you, it's been so difficult to keep in touch with friends.

Worst of all though, are the days spent working alone. Standing in front of a green screen, pretending to talk to others, is like working in a vacuum. This is not what I want to do for a living. I act with people; I don't act on my own.

Apologies for the petulant rant. What right have I to complain when I've chosen to be very well paid to work in a beautiful part of the world? I've had some amazing times; being dropped by a helicopter into virgin snow up to my knees and left to stride across breathtaking mountains, along a perilous ridge: that is exhilarating, as far from a green screen as you can get. However, away from the sunshine and scenery, most of my work is in an empty claustrophobic box, where technicians have replaced all my fellow actors with photographs which light up when they are supposed to be talking to me! I am now acting all on my own without anyone to bounce off. Today was particularly tiring, and embarrassingly I forgot my microphone was still on. Thinking I was just talking to myself, I actually said out loud, "This is not why I became an actor." To my horror, this was accidentally broadcast across the studio and so I am sitting rather tearfully in my trailer writing to you. [1] *You see to me acting is the perfect career as you get older as it's just so very sociable. On every theatre production, I'm reunited with old friends, and I meet new ones and so geriatrics like me get to work with interesting young people who respect us for our skill and experience. The truth is this green screen filming has made me feel pretty miserable, almost to the point where I've thought perhaps, the time has come for me to stop acting altogether.*[2]

Our director Peter has been very sympathetic, he could see I was unhappy and so just the other day the crew staged an impromptu "Gandalf Appreciation Day" and decorated my tent with props from the Lord of the Rings films. That was a really generous touch when he is so busy, however, it still doesn't stop me feeling isolated when I'm back on set talking to cardboard! Loneliness was never part of my career plan. I know so many of my fellow countrymen have willingly emigrated to this wonderful land and I do love the friendly people here but even though they have Marmite it's simply not quite home or not where I've chosen to feel at home.

So what I am writing to let you know is that, far from being a distraction as you have worried, in many ways thinking about the questions your family research has raised, has really helped keep me going and I genuinely want to find some answers with you as soon as I finally get back home from this Unexpected Journey.

I've been thinking over many of the things Grandma Gigi has told us and the one saying that sticks in my mind the most is "better to have less thunder in the mouth and more lightning in the hand" or as my granny would have said, "Action speaks louder than words." I have come to realise that after all our messaging and calls, now is the time to invite you and Grandma Gigi to England. You need to find out more about your ancestor's homeland, so I have decided that as soon as filming is finished here, I am going to send you tickets to come and visit, and I won't take no for an answer.

And about those family secrets, which Gigi has kept close to her heart all these years, now really is the time to tell your story to the world and for once I think it will be heard. A yearning to belong is what drives us all. I lived with a secret about who I really was, for far too long. It was a heavy burden but once I told the truth the relief was incredible. Honesty, honesty, honesty is always for the best, so whatever support you need I am here for you.

Life is a series of interconnected events but you don't see the significance until you look back. Perhaps you should keep a diary of your discoveries and with Gigi's help write your tale so the world can read all about what your family has known for centuries. The past never really dies, a lot may be forgotten but it lives on in flesh and blood, through the stories our families tell each other. No one should ever be isolated because of who they are, we all just want to be accepted as an authentic part of the world, possibly different, defiantly unique but equal just as we are. Remember, you are the story and the storyteller and stories are what bring human beings together.

And knowing what we have shared on our journey of discovery over this last year, and how your family has kept secrets for over 400 years, I think I can safely confide in you about a Shakespearean role that I have been asked to perform at a major event in London later this year. It will be a real feather in my cap but I won't give you any more clues except to say it has significant meaning for us both. No more words will pass my lips until we meet!

Looking forward to catching up soon

Ian

or as Gigi has labelled me

your

Ahanu[3]

Dear Sir Ian,

Apologies, I still don't feel right calling you anything else but Grandma insists you are Ahanu, the man who laughs, because every time the two of you chat you always end up in hysterics. Have faith in your inner mischief maker, he is still there and we both hate to think of you being miserable.

But I do understand that feeling of loneliness you describe. However, for me, that was how I felt in my own home town. I was lonely and isolated at school despite being in crowds of people. There was no one I could really talk to, who could really understand me, so I never felt I truly belonged and it wasn't until I left for college and moved to a different city that I have begun to feel truly at home in myself. Of course, my family are home, but if you feel the larger community that you live in doesn't accept you as you are, it does create a sense of isolation and that's why I have found Savannah to be a place where I can finally relax.

As you know, Grandma is always relaxed or gives a very good impression of it. She doesn't seem to care what anyone else thinks of her as she is certain of her own place in the world and she has assured me that at this moment what you need is to hear a good joke. So to remind you of her sense of humour this is her yarn for you today:

One Sunday, sitting on the side of the highway waiting to catch speeding drivers, a State Police Officer noticed a car travelling at 22 mph. Considering the slow car as dangerous as a speeder, he turned on his lights and pulled the driver over.

Approaching the car, he noticed five little old Indian ladies in the car, wide-eyed and appearing horrified. The driver, obviously confused, says to him, "Officer, I don't understand, I was doing exactly the speed limit, and I ALWAYS go exactly the speed limit. What seems to be the problem?" "Ma'am," the officer replies, "you weren't speeding, but you should know that driving slower than the speed limit can also be a danger to other drivers." "Slower than the speed limit? No Sir, I was doing the speed limit exactly! Twenty-two miles an hour!" the old Indian woman said proudly.

The State Police officer then explained to her that "22" was the route number, not the speed limit. A bit embarrassed, the woman grinned and thanked the officer for pointing out her error. "But before I let you go, Ma'am, I have to ask . . . Is everyone in this car OK? These women seem awfully shaken and they haven't muttered a single peep this whole time," the officer asks with concern.

"Oh, they'll be all right, officer. We just got off Route 119." [4]

I hope that makes you smile and, knowing Grandma, you will probably guess that, like me, she is very excited about the trip to England; in fact, she was jumping up and down when I told her. You are so generous and kind, and without your genuine interest and help, I don't think we'd ever have known where to look for the final pieces of our family jigsaw.

I have started to write some notes about all the characters in the story, from what I've learned so far. A year ago they would have just felt like characters in a play. Many things are on the outside of your experience as you are growing up. You are dimly aware of the history of your family, but you don't know all the facts and you don't think to ask simply because it is family and your own flesh and blood are as familiar as your own reflection. As a child, you just accept your relatives, warts and all. They just are; you live and breathe together without asking, how did you get to be who you are? Ancestors can seem abstract people but when you begin to understand the detail, then they become real, and you feel the flesh and blood connection, you don't just want to know more, you have to know more. So now I know there is a real connection, that they are family and friends, I feel as you say, obligated to tell the truth about my journey of discovery. Every family has its own secrets; it's just that ours go back a little further than most.

However, in terms of telling the story, as you have been so much a part of it, I feel it has to start with the day we first met. Let me know your thoughts about my first attempts at recording how it all began and attached are brief notes on the main characters.

Thanks

Taylor

CAST OF CHARACTERS

William Bradford (1590–1647) - A Yorkshire farmer's son, who lost both parents and sister whilst very young, William turned to William Brewster a separatist leader and Puritan preacher, as a father figure. This did not please his uncles, who were his guardians until he was old enough to inherit his farm. He had never even left his home county when he fled to Holland in 1607 as a teenager, to escape religious persecution with the Brewster family. Working as a weaver in Leiden, he was married with a young son John when the group decided to flee further persecution by sailing to America in 1620. He travelled on *The Mayflower* with his wife, who died before they landed and left his son back in Holland with his wife's grandparents until **John Bradford** was old enough to travel to America on his own. William was chosen as the leader of the Plymouth Colony in Massachusetts and started to write *Of Plymouth Plantation* a decade after they landed and finished the work 21 years later in 1651. The book is regarded as the most authoritative account of the Pilgrims and the early years of the Colony they founded, and in it, he makes it very clear how much the group relied on Squanto the Indian for their survival and how it was a genuine friendship.

Squanto (1588 tbd–1622) - An elite warrior of the Algonquin people of Eastern Massachusetts with unique abilities and stamina, Squanto's full warrior name is Tisquantum. Not only had this native Indian crossed the Atlantic more times than any of the Pilgrims, but he was also probably one of the most well-travelled people in America at this time. Of the journeys that are recorded we know that he lived and worked in Europe, specifically London, Plymouth and Malaga as well as working in Newfoundland. Sponsored by courtiers, who would have known The King's Men, it is most probable that he helped inspire the themes of *The Tempest*. There are many corroborated accounts of Squanto's experiences as a multi-trip visitor across the Atlantic, including the notes of **Sir Ferdinando Gorges** the military Governor of Plymouth Harbour. He wrote about Squanto being part of a group of five Indians brought to him in 1605 by Captain Weymouth, which he then used to persuade King James to allow settlement of America. The Plymouth Company—an English joint-stock company founded in 1606 by James I with the purpose of establishing settlements on the coast of North America—was run by Sir Ferdinando Gorges and Shakespeare's patron and lifelong friend the Earl of Southampton.

Epenow (Contemporary of Squanto) - Like Squanto, he too had been kidnapped by the English but rather than work with them, he decided to actively work against them. Epenow had been used as a "wonder" a spectacle on constant public display in London. Such was the disgust with the way he was treated on his return to America he escaped and became an important source of anti-English resistance when the Plymouth colonists arrived six years later. In the summer just before the Pilgrims arrived he attacked a peaceful coastal mapping voyage that Squanto was helping with. Squanto helped his English Captain Thomas Dermer escape, but was then taken captive by Epenow and handed over to Chief Massasoit. Nevertheless, it was Squanto's arguments that won the day during the winter pow-wow held to discuss the fate of the Pilgrims, and Squanto led the peace discussions.

Massasoit (1581–1661) - The local Chief or Sachem was the paramount chief of the Wampanoag tribe democratically chosen by the tribe to be the leader. Whilst Squanto was in Europe, the Wampanoag suffered from a series of epidemics, which many believe were viruses unknown to North America that arrived with European explorers and decimated as much as 90% of the population, particularly in the Patuxet area which was Squanto's home. When the Pilgrims landed in Patuxet, the area was littered with skeletons as the virus was so deadly people had simply died where they fell. Squanto managed to persuade Massasoit to seek an alliance with the English and their guns to strengthen his weakened hand against the neighbouring Narragansett tribe, who had not been hit by smallpox and were now a much bigger threat than a small group of English visitors.

Myles Standish (1584–1656) - A military man with a reputation for brutality and proactive action: his tendency to violence disturbed more moderate members of the colony. Born in Lancashire, he served as a soldier of fortune in the Low Countries, and his military expertise and devotion to the colony's survival made him an indispensable member of the Pilgrim community. Known as "Captain Shrimpe" by his detractors he was short, had red hair and a fiery temper. He was thin-skinned and quick to take umbrage at the smallest slight. He never trusted the Indians and always sought to strike first. He tended to Bradford during his illness that first winter and William credited him with saving his life. But they were opposites; William patient and slow of judgment while Standish was well known for his short fuse. Whilst William has a strong relationship with Squanto, Myles befriends Hobbamock.

Hobbamock Known for his rivalry with Squanto was also an elite warrior (pniese) of the Pokanoket Tribe of the Wampanoag. Both Hobbamock and Squanto were named after Indian spirits, and it was said a pniese could not be killed in battle and they were responsible for collecting tributes for their Sachem. Hobbamock was Massasoit's right-hand man and became a foot soldier for Myles Standish, living alongside the Plymouth camp and actively spying on and getting involved in battles against rival tribes.

Sir Ferdinando Gorges (1568–1647) Cousin of Sir Walter Raleigh, was knighted on the battlefield in France by the Earl of Essex and appointed by Elizabeth I as commander of Plymouth Fort. He was removed from this post when he was unwillingly drawn into the Earl of Essex's rebellion but made a good friend in Sir John Popham, whom he helped to rescue. He regained his command of Plymouth fort on the accession of James I and uses his friendship with Sir John Popham who is now Chief Justice to get the King's permission to create the Plymouth Company.

William Shakespeare (1564–1616) - "*The Past is Prologue,*" a quote from *The Tempest,* is engraved on the National Archives Building in Washington, D.C. The play has always been seen as a drama inspired by the discoveries in

America but what if Shakespeare had met some Native Americans himself? It is clear from the circles he moved in and the pubs he'd frequent that William would have heard first-hand many traveller's tall tales. Shakespeare's working life was in Southwark, south of the river, and London Bridge, a dangerous district, free of the City of London's rules, but home to its theatres, pleasure gardens, bear-fighting pits, taverns, and brothels. Historical records provide proof of this area being home to many different nationalities so in a very literal sense, Shakespeare knew people of colour. He walked through their neighbourhoods every day. At the same time, he was also very familiar at court as his troupe The King's Men performed for King James twice as often as they did for Queen Elizabeth.

Chapter One

PAST IS PROLOGUE

It's difficult to say what triggered it. The sound of a ringtone like the one I used to have? Or was it a car backfiring and someone pushing past me wearing combat trousers just like his? Whatever the cause, I was now in full flight mode, cold sweat down my back, that horrific metallic taste, stomach churning and legs wobbling. I can see him framed in the doorway of the classroom, cropped hair, *Clockwork Orange* make-up and a gun loaded and aimed. All my schoolmates abandon me, they know his target and they are screaming as they run away. He fires and everything is in slow motion and silent as if the mute button has been pressed. I watch the bullet coming toward me. I know I have to sit down. So that's how I found myself in Leopold's, going through the drill; anchor, breathe, and ask the five questions.

Breathe. What five things can I see?

An old-fashioned café and soda fountain, probably a hundred years old, there's a wooden counter and shelves, black and white tiles on the floor, staff in maroon aprons, white hats and American flags flying above the menu.

Breathe. What four things can I touch?

A marble tabletop cooling and smooth on the fingers the arch of the wooden chair in my back, a firm metal spoon and a china plate.

Breathe. What three things can I hear?

Lots of customer chatter, the clank of knives and forks on dishes and above that in louder voices the sound of orders being made.

Breathe. What can I smell?

Butter pecan ice cream and freshly brewed coffee.

Breathe. What can I taste?

Peanut butter and jelly sandwich, with added banana.

I was back in the room: the peanut butter had done the job, and memories of school were receding behind the overwhelming aroma of coffee. This was not just any room, this was an assault to the senses that was Leopold's; a Savannah tradition. Established by European immigrants last century, today it feels more American than apple pie, but maybe that afternoon I was lingering just a little too long, staring at all the classic movie posters to take my mind off things I never wanted to remember again. Now it had started to rain and as I gingerly stepped outside to shelter under the canopy of the Trustee Theatre next door, I was regretting thinking it wasn't cool for a student to carry an umbrella. Even though my lecture was only across the street, this deluge would mean an afternoon in soggy clothes. Amongst the reasons I'd chosen to study at the Art College here, apart from wanting to get away from home, was that it was everything Plymouth wasn't. The freedom of moving to a city where you become a stranger means you can finally feel comfortable in your own skin and don't have to stick to the role others have chosen for you. My mind was able to roam and shape my own future away from a past that at home was cemented to my shoes. To me, this city felt warm and friendly, even in the rain and not only that, they ran a great film festival.[1] Together Leopold's and the nostalgic Trustee theatre next door was like a slice of very comforting 1950s Americana, feeding that yearning we all have for simpler days. As the rain continued to pour, I stared at Liam Neeson's poster with regret. I had meant to see his talk the night before but as usual, had left it too late to get a ticket. Now I was going to be late again and just as I had decided I needed to run, the door swung open, and the usher looked at me accusingly, "Well, if you are coming in, get a move on." It was a simple choice either get wet and then potentially bored or sit inside, stay dry and be entertained. I didn't hesitate. As I quietly snuck into the last seat, out walked Gandalf, and I was transfixed.

I'm maybe the last actor alive to say that I was the first to create a role written by William Shakespeare. There is a manuscript in the British Museum[2] which pre-dates the arrival of The Pilgrim Fathers to America. Specialists who have studied this Elizabethan play know it was written around 1590 but then later revised and in it, there is a speech for Thomas More written by a Hand D. The many experts who have looked at it believe it to have been the work of William Shakespeare. Presuming they are correct, this folio is the only surviving example of a text in Shakespeare's own handwriting. But I believe it is special, not just because of who wrote it, but because of what he wrote. Hand D's speech for Thomas More couldn't be more relevant about the question of refugees, and it is striking that right at the birth of modern Britain, Shakespeare makes a strong case that "the majesty of England" depends not on keeping them out, but on taking them in.[3]

The scene I'm going to read you is based on a real historical event, the "Ill May Day" of May 1st, 1517. A mob of working-class apprentices had gathered in the middle of London in what is now known as Trafalgar Square, planning to burn the houses of the city's growing immigrant community. Many of these immigrants were political and religious refugees from France, Belgium, and Italy. Thomas More, then Under-Sheriff of London, is sent out by the authorities to put the riot down and he does it by appealing to their sense of good behaviour and as is written in this speech by Shakespeare an appeal to their humanity.

And I might just say because it is relevant—that just last year in October a middle-aged man who had been unemployed for some time had just got a job and was out in this very part of London with his civil partner celebrating. A group of three teenagers, two girls, and a boy recognised them as being gay and started insulting them—he riposted verbally, and they kicked him, and then one of the girls stamped on his head until he was dead.[8] I tell you this because it happened in my city, in my country and our world and the speech I'm going to get round to doing for you takes place just where that man was killed only a year ago.

So back to this speech, there's a crowd out on the street, and they are complaining about the strangers in their midst—immigrants really, people of different colour, different culture, different food, they come over here they take our jobs, take our women ... you know ... send them back home *"strangers should be removed"* is the cry from the crowd and this is how Thomas More responds ...

> *"Grant them removed, and grant that this your noise*
> *Hath chid down all the majesty of England;*
> *Imagine that you see the wretched strangers,*
> *Their babies at their backs with their poor luggage,*
> *Plodding to the ports and coasts for transportation,*
> *And that you sit as kings in your desires,*
> *Authority quite silent by your brawl,*
> *And you in ruff of your opinions clothed;*
> *What had you got? I'll tell you: you had taught*
> *How insolence and strong hand should prevail,*
> *How order should be quelled; and by this pattern*
> *Not one of you should live an aged man,*
> *For other ruffians, as their fancies wrought,*
> *With self-same hand, self-reasons, and self-right,*
> *Would shark on you, and men like ravenous fishes*
> *Would feed on one another ... You'd put down strangers ... kill*
> *them, cut their throats........*
> *Say now the king ... Should so much come too short of your great*
> *trespass*
> *As but to banish you, whither would you go?*
> *What country, by the nature of your error,*
> *Should give you harbour? Go you to France or Flanders,*
> *To any German province, to Spain or Portugal,*

Nay, anywhere that not adheres to England,
Why, you must needs be strangers: would you be pleased
To find a nation of such barbarous temper,
That, breaking out in hideous violence,
Would not afford you an abode on earth,
Whet their detested knives against your throats,
Spurn you like dogs, and like as if that God
Owed not nor made not you, nor that the elements
Where not all appropriate to your comforts,
But chartered unto them, what would you think
To be thus used? This is the stranger's case; And this your moun-
tainish inhumanity."

Apart from the fact that this was the first time I'd ever been so close to an actor who can make words that make no sense to me on the page just come alive and sound as if they were written yesterday—I was transfixed by the image behind him. The combination of the beautiful words and a slide of an old yellowing manuscript in ancient handwriting with damp stains and crossings out was making my legs wobble again, but this time it wasn't fear but something even odder, familiarity. And as I sat and listened to the mellow McKellen mouth pour Shakespeare into my ears, I knew with a gut certainty that I had seen handwriting like that before. Indeed I'd grown up with it and had been told all my life it was written by one of my ancient relatives who had come over on *The Mayflower*.

Sir Ian's presentation was followed by a question and answer session, and despite knowing I should really keep a low profile for missing class, I found myself putting my hand up.

"Is that script really the only example of Shakespeare's handwriting?"

"Well, I'm not an archivist or an expert in this field but those who are, say apart from this page there are only six other signatures that we know for certain belong to Shakespeare. There are for example those on his will, the deeds to purchase his house and then one from a court case. Anything else is guesswork. William Shakespeare's life story is almost invisible, unlike his dramatic legacy which simply grows bigger every century."

The questions continued mostly about Sir Ian's film career, but I couldn't remove the niggling feeling that I knew this handwriting, but in my family, it belongs to a very different story. I had to ring home ... I sneaked to the back of the hall.

"Taylor, to what do we owe the pleasure? Don't tell me you've run out of money already?"

"No, Ma, strangely enough, I haven't, but I wanted to ask you a question about Grandma."

"Really, well, you could always ask her yourself?"

"Yes, but I want to know the truth and not just the story of the day."

"Well, what makes you think I know the truth?"

"Well, if she's told the same story enough times then maybe there could be something in it."

"Okay, so what's the question?"

"You know in her room there's that picture which Grandma says is one of our ancient relatives and on the back there's some old handwriting."

"Yes."

"Well, what did she tell you about it?"

"Well, the story she always told me was that Great, Great, Great Whatever Grandfather William Bradford, who came over on *The Mayflower*, handed this picture to his children and that it was of his good friend and he'd written something nice about him on the back of the picture."

"Oh?"

"What's the problem?"

"Well, that's exactly the story she told me."

"Well, there you go."

"Is Kirsten there?"

"So I don't even get a ... 'How are you, Ma? The dogs okay?' Just pass me on to the sister I love to tease."

"Look, Ma, sorry, I'm just in a rush, I promise I will not yank her chain."

"Okay, so as long as you're fine and you're still coming back for Thanksgiving?"

"Wouldn't dare miss it."

"Kirsten, look, big favour, I owe you one—Ma wouldn't understand, but I've just skipped a class to listen to Sir Ian McKellen—yes, you know Gandalf—and I really need to show him something. Please, could you just go into the study and take a picture of the writing on the back of that old painting Grandma has on her desk."

"Why?"

"Look, he's going to go in a minute, don't ask why, please just do, and I'll owe you a wicked Water Street breakfast when we get back … yes, the works … thanks."

Kirsten might be annoying but offering a stack of pancakes as a bribe was going to be far easier than trying to explain to Ma how to send me a photo on her phone quickly.

I could see the queue for autographs was thinning out, and Sir Ian was about to be ushered away so I plucked up my courage and got to the end of the line, and then security stepped in.

"No more now—it's a long way back to Hobbit town in New Zealand, you know?"

"Yes, but I don't want an autograph, I just want to show Sir Ian something."

Sir Ian gestured magnanimously towards me and as he did my phone pinged with the evidence I needed.

"Thank you, Sir; I just wanted to show you a picture it's on my phone."

Sir Ian adjusts his glasses looks down and then looks up at me quizzically.

"That's very interesting …?"

"Oh, no, sorry, not the picture, it's what's written on the back … here."

"…*more gentle-kind than of our human generation you shall find, many, nay, almost any.* I believe *The Tempest*, Act 3, Scene 3."

"So it is Shakespeare?"

"Certainly."

"And does it look like the writing on your screen?"

Sir Ian turns around and looks between the giant projection of his Thomas More folio and the tiny screen on my phone of the brown paper sealed at the back of my Grandma's painting.

"Fascinating … where is this from?"

"Well, it's been in my family forever, but we were always told it was written by one of our relatives, another William, William Bradford."

"I do have to catch a plane but can we keep in touch—can we swap numbers?"

What was that song Ma likes? "*A star fall, a phone call, It joins all, Synchronicity.*"

If it wasn't for the rain that day and an empty seat …. I wouldn't have Gandalf's phone number.

PLYMOUTH, MASSACHUSETTS, THANKSGIVING, NOVEMBER 25TH, 2010

And so for the unexpected guest who would point me on an unexpected journey. I had forwarded on Kirsten's badly framed photograph of the writing on the back of the old portrait to Sir Ian and just presumed he was being polite and in a rush to get away. I wasn't going to ring and make small talk and wouldn't know how to with a knight of the realm but when I got a text a few weeks later asking: "Are you free next Thursday?" I did wonder if my chain was now being yanked. I sent a polite note back saying it's Thanksgiving, and I'm with my family, he just responded: "I'm seeing friends in Boston, can I pop over?"

So not thinking he was serious, I'd casually mentioned to Ma that a professor from college might be popping by after dinner to look at Grandma's picture and nothing more was said.

And then he turned up at the door just like Gandalf, and I felt as nervous as Bilbo Baggins. How was this scene going to play out?

"So sorry to impose but you see I am going to be away filming in New Zealand for the next year and just couldn't get your picture and that handwriting out of my head—am I allowed to see it?"

Here was my first problem in order to see it, we had to go into Grandma territory, and it really depended on her mood.

"Of course, as long as you don't mind talking to Grandma?" I tried to warn him with a carefully raised eyebrow, but then nothing can prepare you for Grandma in full flow. "She's a bit of an old hippy—my Ma was born at Woodstock—imagine a small Cher with plaits but without the plastic surgery or hair dye."

"Well, then we've clearly got a lot in common as we must be around the same age."

"And she's always surrounded by books because of all her 'family research.'"

"Is that you, Weetamoo?"[9] Gigi called out from her study and now Sir Ian's eyebrows raised, and I shrug my shoulders and nod and with a cringe admit.

"Family nickname …. Yes, Gigi, I'm here with the teacher I told you about."

I open the door to Gigi's room, who you can barely spot behind a desk overloaded with books and journals piled high along, over and around her bare feet.

"Oh, yes, the Shakespeare expert, have I met you before? I do feel I know you?"

Sir Ian could not have been more gracious.

"No, Madam, but I'm sure now we have, that we'll meet again."

Big smiles all 'round.

"My name is Ougina, but you can call me Gigi. And your name?"

"Ian."

"Well, Ian, that's a nice short name already, Weetamoo tells me you want to know about the miniature portrait?"

"I'm all ears."

"Well, make yourself comfortable." Gigi throws a pile of papers off the nearest chair and beckons him to take the weight off his feet—so that he'll be a little closer in height to his host.

"It all started a long time ago but as my mother used to say, '*What's gone and what's past help, should be past grief.*'"[10]

"Clearly your family loves a good Shakespearean quote."

"Really, I thought it was just an old Pilgrim saying—my mum and her mum were always using it."

"Well, that may well be, but in my world, Shakespeare gave those words to Paulina, Queen Hermione's friend from *The Winter's Tale.* "

"Well, never knew that. Anyway, the short version of the story behind this picture is quite simple. It was handed down in my family from mother to mother and is nearly 400 years old and dates back to the arrival of *The Mayflower.* Our family can trace its ancestry back to William Bradford, and this picture is of his dearest friend and I was told this is what he wrote about him. Also, it does look like the writing in his book *Of Plymouth Plantation* and we know in that book he wrote that Squanto '*was a special instrument sent of God for their good beyond their expectation.*'"

Sir Ian turns to me. "Did you know all this, Taylor, when you showed it to me?"

Grandma looks hurt.

"Sorry, Gigi, but you've told me so many stories I'm never sure which ones are true. Yes, I thought that was the story but then realised it probably best you heard it from the expert."

"The expert?"

"Yes, well, I have spent some time researching family links so if you want the long version—and have a few hours to spare—then I can fill you in on the detail—warts and all."

"Well, my flight's not until the weekend—so I'm all yours."

"Weetamoo—you can make a packie run."[11]

"Are you sending Taylor away?"

"Only to get the drinks in!"

"Oh, good. Before we start then, as I told Taylor I'm not really an expert more of a Shakespeare specialist, but one thing I do know is that the Puritans like your ancestor William Bradford were not really fans of the theatre. In fact, they strongly objected to places like The Globe because of the somewhat 'bawdy' nature of some of the plays, well, that along with the fighting and copious drinking."

Sir Ian jumps from his chair as he notices I'm stuck in the door with a wobbling tray filled with a selection of Gigi's finest.

"Oh, Taylor, let me help you with that drinks tray—this now looks like a great evening of storytelling is on its way—Cheers!"

Drinks are poured, and we all settle into comfy chairs, as if for a cosy night at Bag End.

"So, as I was explaining to Gigi, the thing is, London theatres in Shakespeare's day were probably some of the most unruly places in the city, and Puritans like William Bradford would have done all they could to avoid them as they saw drama as an abomination and a snare. They were the sort of people who wanted to stop bear-baiting not because it gave pain to the bear but because it gave pleasure to the spectator.[12] So knowing that was their thinking, I'm just surprised that one of the Pilgrim Fathers would have brought knowledge of Shakespeare across the ocean."

"Well, that's why I need to tell you the whole story as maybe it's not quite how it seems and you'll find that you really can't get there from here."

"As the good bard would say, '*What's past is prologue, what to come, in yours and my discharge.*'"

So it was that Gandalf and Grandma came to be friends and my life would never be the same again.

NEW ZEALAND,
FEBRUARY 2012

Taylor,

I have to say that is a very flattering account of our first encounter but make sure you have also got Gigi's approval—especially on the size of the drinks tray!

What I was thinking of, though, was that maybe you could write about the *Mayflower* story from the very beginning. Now you've read *Of Plymouth Plantation* and heard all those stories from Gigi, why don't you start by writing a diary of the events leading up to the Pilgrims' arrival in America? Imagine you are walking in your ancestors' footsteps and how that journey might have felt—I've attached a link to Yorkshire dialect which might prove useful.

SAVANNAH, GEORGIA,
FEBRUARY 2012

Dear Sir Ian,

This is all new to me, I'm not sure I am up to the task, but I made a start today. I woke up this morning with two vivid scenes playing in my head both happening on the same day but either side of the Atlantic, and it feels like they need to be linked together, so rather than tackle my art history essay I sketched these out—what do you think?

PLYMOUTH, DEVON,
SEPTEMBER 6TH, 1620 – WILLIAM BRADFORD'S VIEW

It still looked choppy out at sea, but the Captain said it was time to set sail. I stepped down from the firm cold cobbles of Sutton Harbour to the rocking of the wooden deck, I had to cramble just to stand still.[13] Trying to stand firm on a surface that had other thoughts, was a challenge and as I looked longingly back at the harbour wall, after all our false starts, I was now worried that those really were my last steps on English ground and that I would never find my sea legs!

I know the Speedwell crew had sabotaged their ship; I overheard them talking about the dangers of a voyage this late in the year, and they are the experts, but we have put our faith in God, the problem is, can we trust our Captain Jones to be faithful and true?

We had watched over the last month as ships had come in and out of harbour and to be truthful many more were coming in than out. A lot of the ships coming in were already returning from America, they were the ships with the most distinctive smell which we discovered was salted cod, an aroma and taste that we would become all too familiar with.

No sooner are we out of harbour than the swell and the movement of Atlantic gales confirm that nothing has changed, I still feel as violently ill as ever, my stomach will not rest from gipping, God help me, this will be one long noggling crossing.[14]

CAPE COD,
SEPTEMBER 6TH, 1620 – SQUANTO'S VIEW

When it happens, you realise you already know what your own blood tastes of.

"Why, Epenow, why? He is a good man like the English gentleman that rescued you. Let him go."

Epenow's face was painted red and black for battle, there was nothing to reason with as he shrieked his loudest war cry in my face.

"This is for all the English men that betrayed both me and you. I cannot let any of them go. They are here to destroy us, I have dreamt it, I know it and you need to let go. Save yourself before it's too late. He dies, Squanto."

And the blunt edge of Epenow's axe drops again onto my head until I fall backward onto the ship's wooden deck and into darkness.

NEW ZEALAND, FEBRUARY 2012

Dear Taylor,

Noggling is a grand Yorkshire word, I think this is a great start but what I actually meant timewise was going back even further to the start of all the events leading up to The Mayflower's departure, even Bradford's childhood maybe? Why don't you pick a date before William had even thought of leaving his own village?

SAVANNAH, GEORGIA, FEBRUARY 2012

Dear Sir Ian,

Unbelievably, I have been reading history books about all those early days, without falling asleep. Indeed, now I have a vested interest, I am finding them really interesting, so last night I decided to pick the date we met and just dial the clock back 400 years. Nothing came to mind immediately so I read some more, thought about what those times must have felt like, slept on it and then when I woke the English and American images where just as vivid as before, it seems I can't think of one without the other.

AUSTERFIELD, YORKSHIRE,
NOVEMBER 4TH, 1604 — BRADFORD'S VIEW

It was a cold backend night under a frosty moon. Carefully I placed a bolster under my covers, so even if my uncles did look in, it would appear as if I was sleeping. As I crept out of the window, I knew I would be able to see my way from our farm across the fields to Mr. Brewster's manor house. I'd been forbidden to meet or talk to Mr. Brewster, even if he had worked for the Queen, my uncles saw his being a reformist as a dangerous thing. If our church is good enough for the new King, then it's good enough for us was their argument, anything for a quiet life. But Mr. Brewster was a clever man, maybe he wasn't much of a tyke now, but that's because he'd studied at Cambridge and spent time in the lowlands but he's Scrooby born and more importantly for me, he was happy to lend books. His arguments about how to reform the church were always carefully considered, not like my uncles whose arguments always ended with, "Don't be a bedlamite, William, 'appen you'll do as we say!" they are fair wittlers. Yet as I walked through the puddles along the ginnel, I knew they were right about how things had changed since James had become King. There was talk of how he wanted to stop any church reform and so that was why we were now meeting in secret, for fear of imprisonment. Whatever the punishment, though, I couldn't stop, wouldn't stop no matter what my uncles or the King might say—this congregation was my family now, my home, this is where I belong.

CAPE COD,
NOVEMBER 4TH, 1604 — SQUANTO'S VIEW

I'd seen them before but never this close. My father had told me of seeing many dozens of anchored clouds that travelled past our bay, this one though had chosen to stop. [15] Carefully hidden behind a dune, I watched as the cloud stopped offshore. The pale strangers stepped from under the cloud into a fat, slow canoe and rowed slowly across the cove. As they walked on to the beach, even from a tree trunk away you could smell them, rancid body odour, bristly faced creatures; they can't have washed for weeks. Then one of them sneezed, but he didn't turn away, instead, he put his nose into a stained cloth and put it back into his breeches. Strange beings, to keep something close to them that their bodies choose to reject. Massasoit, our chief has said we can't even be sure they are human. Their skin is always covered with cloth apart from their hands and face and that combined with their icy stares and strange behaviour, made us keep our distance. They don't seem to care for each other, and those we've watched always seem to end up shouting or fighting. Clearly, they were made of blood and sweat, that smell was best not to dwell on, but we hadn't seen any tears, and there was no way to tell if they cared for each other? There seemed to be no kinship, and we never saw any women or children. But the hairy men were talking now, the words came fast and furious I couldn't read the sounds, but I sensed both anger and fear. This was the moment when a group of geese decided to fly directly over my hiding place. There is no way the hairy ones can miss this noise, it sounds like a tempest as they flap low across the bay and of course the group turn directly towards me. I could see one of them had the "peskunck," the thunder stick we'd been told about and with his piercing blue eyes, he must have seen me by now. The noise of the fire blast and goose squawks are not something I'll forget in a hurry. One explosion and three geese were falling towards the beach, feathers falling over my head. This was my cue to disappear before they saw me; it was dusk and would not be long before the frosty moon appeared. I kept the feathers.

NEW ZEALAND,
FEBRUARY 2012

Taylor,

This is beginning to motor now. And I can see from your notes all the research you've done. Why don't you start a new chapter with William's first journey abroad?

SAVANNAH,
FEBRUARY 2012

It's quite amazing how much you can read in such a short space of time when you find something that fascinates. My friends are getting worried as I've disappeared off social media but I'm quite happy in my own bubble, discovering what life was like for my ancestors. Today people get worried if you aren't contactable after a few hours; how would they have survived knowing that travelling then meant no contact with family and friends for years? Here you go—my first attempt at Chapter Two— yet again you get two stories for the price of one! Let me know what you think of last night's thoughts plus the stories you heard at your first meeting with Gigi.

Chapter Two

LOVED NOT WISELY BUT TOO WELL

**IMMINGHAM, LINCOLNSHIRE,
OCTOBER 11TH, 1607 –
WILLIAM BRADFORD'S FIRST VOYAGE**

For me, there is simply no choice. William Brewster and John Robinson are now my family. When the Bishop of York imprisoned them for worshipping the Lord and remaining true to our faith, we knew it was time to leave. We felt hunted and persecuted from every side, and now there was a warrant for Mr. Brewster's arrest, describing him as a dangerous Separatist. King James had made it clear he would "harry" any Puritans out of England and had already executed several. Well, we wanted to go, we know we are not welcome any more but we need official permission to travel abroad, and the authorities refuse to grant us that. So if we are to sail to Holland a place Mr. Brewster knows well, we would have to do it secretly.

My uncles and friends could rail at me all they like, but without a mother, father or sister what was there to keep me here? Yes, at twenty-one I will inherit the farm but that's another four years off and four years without the fellowship is not a life I want to lead. So that was why I was stood on the foggy banks of the Humber in the chill of an autumn evening waiting for a Dutchman to rescue us. The first captain who promised to take us was English, but an Outman, who turned out to be a kallifudging traitor turning us into the authorities in Boston which had meant several more months of jail.

Now here we stood again, in the damp flosh, most of us having never ventured out of Yorkshire, waiting to start a new life abroad. The wisps of fog smelt marshy and hung heavy around our legs like the ghosts of the lives we were leaving behind. The gangplank splashed down, and William and John led the way with a group of us to check all was safe before allowing the women and children on board, and that is when we heard the horses, the local militia were moving in. The captain wasted no time; he had no wish to be caught and was determined to sail for Amsterdam. Without waiting to see who it was, he shouted out orders to his crew in Dutch and before any of the women could be boarded we were already sailing out to sea. William and John shouted out words of encouragement promising to come back, but it was several months before they could keep that promise. I won't forget the sound of the women and children weeping in despair as we floated out into the darkness and as they cried, I suddenly heard the sound of my own cries as a little one when Grandfather told me mother was dead. I am not afraid to admit in the dark of the night I leaned over the ship and let my guts turn inside out.

PATUXET, JUNE 11TH, 1605 —SQUANTO'S FIRST VOYAGE

This time was going to be different, this time I was going to see into their anchored cloud. I wanted to know how it worked, how they made it move, I was ready for my warrior challenge. Last year was my final spirit warrior training if there was a time to walk amongst the strangers it was now. I had spent the winter alone in the forest of wolves. I had shown I can survive the cold, ignore pain, fast and still drink the bitter juice that empties everything even in an empty stomach. I had fasted until my child soul had left, I was now ready to meet them and understand their magic. If these strangers were going to keep on coming to our shores, and maybe stay longer like the hairy white men in the north who come to fish, we had to understand them and how their minds work. I could not speak their language yet but it does not require many words to speak the truth, and I am the quickest in my tribe to understand other tribe talk and can mimic all the sounds of the forest. They were all mostly smaller and didn't look as strong as us, but their strange dress held dangerous tools, knives, and guns that could do great damage. I could hold my own; they looked simply *ntu'tem*—a relative of a strange race—who just didn't happen to wash! Our Sachem said Maushap[1] taught that the world was full of beings, who did as they pleased with no care for others and our role is to teach generosity to these creatures. Many of my tribal elders warned of how these strangers have taken warriors from other tribes and were not to be trusted but then we heard from the Massachusetts tribe the cloud was coming our way, and they only wanted to trade. So now here they were in our harbour, and I was amongst the first to reach the ship.

I could sense the strangers were wary, but they spent a great deal of time trying to explain they wanted to exchange goods. What is interesting when you don't know each other's language yet, is that you can see motive and character that much quicker. Their chief stood back and gauged us whilst his men seemed to use many, many words where we would just use one. They were nervous, but I could see they had their thunder sticks close by for protection and they excitedly offered us their treasures. Some useful and beautiful things, copper kettles, glittering coloured glass, steel knives, and hatchets—unlike anything else we had and they wanted to exchange these valuable items for the furs we used as blankets. It was easy to tell from their eyes they placed a high value on the sable skins, so to play a game, I held back the sable and only offered beaver; this is the point where the Chief stepped in. He wanted to impress us and had a Sachem trick I had seen once before in the north. He touched his sword with a Loadstone, took up a knife, and made the knife turn, by touching it with his sword, then he used it to pick up a needle, my companions made approving noises and I think they imagined we thought they had shown us a great power.[2] But when offered food we did very much enjoy their peas and ale which we hadn't tasted before, and they very much enjoyed our tobacco. We had a pleasant evening, and I offered to stay on board to show that we trusted them and I wanted an opportunity to learn more about them. I could see that their captain was a kind character I wasn't too sure about some of his men, but he seemed to be keen that I stay and travel with them. I was a young warrior and needed my own adventure, as a tribe we needed to know what they really wanted, so I decided it was time to be a feather for each wind that blows and go where this journey would take me.

THANKSGIVING, PLYMOUTH, MASSACHUSETTS, NOVEMBER 25TH, 2010

So with a drink in hand, nestled into her chair, surrounded by a lifetime of research Grandma began to explain our family story to Sir Ian.

My version of the story always starts at the end here in Plymouth. William Bradford who was one of the first to land ashore and appointed Governor for those difficult early years has been ill for weeks and is clearly on his deathbed. It's 1657, he has governed the colony five times over a period of nearly 40 years. His second wife is by his bedside and a large extended family, their children, her children from her first marriage and also a number of orphans they adopted from the early days of the colony—but he's missing someone, his firstborn and eldest son from his first marriage. After John got married, he moved away to Norwich, Connecticut, which at that time was about as far away from Plymouth as it was possible for a New Englander to get. So a messenger is sent to fetch him.

Despite the messenger's pleading John is very reluctant to go and see his father, it's a four-day ride by horse, they haven't spoken for years, he won't have anything new to say and besides, if his father is that ill, then he may have died before he even arrives. This is obviously a son tired of living in the shadow of his father's "fame" and reputation. Clearly, there is a family rift that had not healed, but his wife Martha decides this is the moment differences have to be forgotten, and she insists he must go.

John sets off and arrives tired and depressed, the journey had only made him angrier at his father for everything that had come between them. At the age of just three, he had been left behind in Holland whilst his mother and father left for America to start a new life. Effectively orphaned he lived with his grandparents, never saw his mother again as she died before they landed and was not allowed to travel across the Atlantic until he was eleven by which point his father had already remarried. And so the longed-for reunion John had so often imagined with his father never really happened. By the time he arrived, he was presented with a new half-brother and sister with another brother on the way and various orphans which meant he was just one of a crowd of at least twelve in a house that was always full of visitors looking for help and guidance. Walking into his father's room this time, there is that same crowd again so that he can't even see his father's face. A hand reaches up from the bed to wave him away, and he's so angry he can't stop himself from shouting out.

PLYMOUTH
1657 – BRADFORD'S DEATHBED

"I've just ridden through the night to see you, and the first thing you do is tell me to go."

"Not you—the others." The crowd leave and William points to the seat next to him.

With great heavy breaths, William heaves himself upright to show John that despite his frailties this is going to be an important conversation.

"I need to tell you, my eldest, the truth, it's time. I need to explain to you why I did what I did and if you can't find it in your heart to forgive me at least, you can understand.

"You were always a much-loved much-wanted child. However, once you were born your mother and I knew that we didn't want to bring you up as a Dutch child. We were living in Leiden, but we were English, and wanted you to have the sort of upbringing we had, and to do that we needed to leave Holland. It was having you that changed our lives, which took us on the journey to our New England. What we didn't know is how many lives it would take to make that new start, and I can't begin to tell you how wretched I am that your mother was one of the many who didn't make it. There isn't a day I haven't thought she should have stayed behind with you until things were safe because I know what the pain of losing your mother is like—I lost my mother and sister when I was just a little one and never even knew my father. She wanted to go back for you as soon as we were in sight of land, but I told her it was impossible. I didn't want you to feel that pain but who are we to question God's plan?"

"Well, you never would."

"No, I wouldn't because although that pain has never gone away, it has made me appreciate all that I have even more and without her loss, we wouldn't now have your brothers and sister. Just look outside at that blossom, every winter the world is covered in snow and in the midst of that cold we can't think that spring will ever come again, but it does and every May the flowers return" ... He takes a heavy breath ... "just smell that honeysuckle."

John sighs feeling as uncomfortable as he always did with his father's utter conviction that his understanding of God's way is the only way.

"You have to understand that we were fighting for our faith. In England, we would have been imprisoned for wanting to worship God directly the way we do here, and God wanted us to go. He sent us a sign just after you were born, a blazing red star with an angry tail appeared in the skies for seven weeks, and we knew then it was time to move on to create our new world.[3] We'd already been thrown out of our own country, but our faith stood us apart from other men, small things may discourage others, that they'd then wish themselves home again.[4] We though, we knew we were Pilgrims, and we took these trials to get here as a test of our faith. We were sixty-six days at sea John with nothing but storms. We'd set off at the wrong time of year, and it was such an old ship, the Captain said it had fought in the Spanish Armada. At one point when one of the main timbers broke, he wanted to turn back but together as a group and with God's guidance, we managed to persuade the Captain that we could repair it. And look at our friend John Howland—he fell off the boat in one of those storms but he clung to the halyard, and together we pulled him in and now he and his wife have ten children."

"But God chose not to save my mother."

"John, half the passengers died that first winter, I very nearly did but those of us who survived, God saved us for a higher purpose—look at Jamestown where the savages massacred everyone. God had cleared the land for us here and placed us next to natives who were happy to share with us, and he gave us one Indian, Squanto who I know now was a special instrument sent of God for our good beyond our expectation.[5]

"As we were leaving Plymouth in Devon, for the second time of trying, the Governor of the Fort there, a Sir Ferdinando Gorges[6] arrived with a letter to show us. It was from one of his Captains: Thomas Dermer,[7] who was already scouting the coast of New England with his translator who was our Squanto. They'd arrived at a place a few months earlier and reported that there had been a terrible plague that had deserted a once populous area. '... *found some ancient Plantations, not long since populous, now utterly void*' was the message.

'*I would that the first plantation might here be seated.*' We weren't meant to land in New Plymouth, but when the winter storms sent us off course we knew then that it was God's plan that we had met with Sir Ferdinando and we knew that right here was a place that God had cleared for us."

"Yes, I know the story, but your promised land was really a '*New Golgotha*'[8] you built your New Plymouth on an old Indian village where the plague hit so hard they hadn't even had time to bury the dead. Your new life came at the cost of their deaths and my mother."

"That may be true. But what you don't know is that Indian village was Squanto's old home. He knew it as Patuxet, but the plague had either killed or driven everyone away. He'd lost everyone he had ever known, but instead of losing faith he joined us and helped us. He chose to join God's mission to create a new home, our new Plymouth and alongside the last of his tribe it also became the burial ground for all the Pilgrims who hadn't made it."

"But not my mother."

Silence falls between the two as William knows he can't say any more to his son about his mother's death. The last conversation they had was just after the *Mayflower* dropped anchor off Cape Cod. William was part of the search party going off to explore the new coast. Dorothy had to stay on board but told him she was missing John and wanted to return, he scolded her, for being foolish. "*Don't wittle woman*" were his last words to her before he went off to explore and on his return, he was told that she had silently fallen into the sea and her body was never found.

PLYMOUTH, MASSACHUSETTS, THANKSGIVING 2010

Sir Ian is visibly moved.

"Who can imagine what Bradford felt that day? They'd made it to the new land, and he loses his wife in sight of their new beginning."

Gigi puts her hand on Sir Ian's.

"But you see, with the Pilgrims faith was everything, they believed God controlled what happened on earth, and they have to live with his will. Dorothy was desperately missing her son, and she disappeared shortly after witnessing a little boy called Jasper dying on board. The only clue William leaves us as to how he felt is a poem he wrote toward the end of his life.

"Faint not, poor soul, in God still trust,
Fear not the things thou suffer must;
For whom he loves he doth chastise,
And then all tears wipes from their eyes.

"Every Biblical text William read reinforced his belief that people were better for the experience of suffering as it made them more worthy of the Kingdom of God. However, William's eldest John is the prodigal son who doesn't want to return home, perhaps his faith is not as unwavering and despite knowing it is his father's deathbed he is still finding it difficult to talk to the father who always put faith before family."

PLYMOUTH, MASSACHUSETTS, 1657 – BRADFORD'S DEATHBED

"Your God always saves the day."

"John, you know he does, even if you pretend to scorn, and we did more than survive: with Squanto's help, we were able to thrive here. He knew the land and what would grow and he taught us all the skills we needed, without him, there is no doubt more of us would have died if not all. And in time we also carefully buried the bones of his old tribe in safe places. You need to understand just how dangerous a place it was before Squanto negotiated and helped to ensure the peace you take for granted. You know that you can walk as peacefully and safely in the woods here as we could back in England and you can entertain the Indians we know here in our homes like friendly neighbours.[9]

However, when we first landed on Cape Cod, we were attacked with bows and arrows, and that first winter was terrifying to live through. We saw many signs of being watched, we had equipment stolen, we saw warriors with bows and arrows on distant hills looking down on us and didn't know what to expect next. Then for three days in February, we knew there was a major gathering in the nearby swamp. All we heard day and night was nothing but horrid loud devilish screams and shouts as if they were trying to curse us all away, or about to start a battle. We'd heard the stories of how others had died—Captain Dermer who had spent the last year travelling the coast was attacked even with Squanto as his translator which is why we brought Myles Standish our military advisor."

"So God could bless the Indians with your gun powder."

"You have to understand: we came in peace, but we knew that it wasn't always guaranteed, and we weren't to know we would find an Indian, who not only spoke fluent English, but could translate all the tribal languages in the area and persuade them all to work with us."

"But how did Squanto know English so well?"

"Because, John, he lived in England longer than you ever have."

PATUXET POWWOW, FEBRUARY 1621 — SQUANTO'S VIEW

The Powwow has just begun and, without waiting to be asked, Epenow breaks ranks and stands firmly on the talking spot hurling his invective towards me.

"The strangers should be removed."

Epenow is dressed in his warrior feathers with the same furious expression he gave me as I stood protecting Captain Dermer whilst he and his tribe attacked us both.

"Why should we let them come? Why should we let them take our land and bring their plagues? We don't need them and their filthy ways, we need to reclaim our country before they steal it away from us. I have lived with them, and I know what they are like, I have seen visions of them deliberately setting our homes on fire. Squanto can use all the fine arguments he likes but they are not like us and they don't understand our ways, and we need to ensure we keep what is ours. They need to be cursed away from here, and I vow to fight. We have been watching them, many are ill and enfeebled so now is the time to strike whilst they are weakened."

Massasoit the Chief turns to me. "We took you in, Squanto, and we don't know what to do with you. You left us many seasons ago and return a different Squanto you now speak their language understand their ways, sail on their ships and work with them. Why should we let them take our sacred home-land? Indeed how could you be happy with them living in the village where you grew up?"

That was my cue to stand on the talking spot.

"But who does the land belong to? Our land is sacred, yes, but we have all been taught land is like air, it is only ours whilst we use it then we pass it on. This land does not belong to us; it's more that we belong to this land. My tribe no longer exists, there is no one but myself that belongs to this land, and I am happy to share with these people as I know what they are really like and I lived with them far longer than Epenow. You know they have muskets and their ships' cannons, you know how much damage they can do, and yet they are here now with women and children and have only fired warning shots. They come with babies on their backs; they have carried their belongings across the great ocean. They come to settle not to make war. But if they wanted to dam-age you, they wouldn't need to fire their thunder sticks they would just release the silent plague that ravaged Patuxet and all those other villages you know that have suffered. Do you want a death so quick that no one in your tribe can have a proper burial?

"Epenow, you are quick to talk war: why do you always think violence is the answer? You know more than the others here how they can respond to our arrows with guns and cannons that can blast a warrior in half. How many of us here would die for your pride when we could all live alongside each other in peace? Massasoit, the Wampanoag are now the weakest tribe in the area, and yet if you ally yourself with these white people, you could become the strongest. Make friends with them and enemies that are now too strong for you, will then have to bow down to you. This is a battle you cannot win, these people will keep on coming, and there are many more of them. Epenow will vouch for that; he lived in their city of London he knows how many more of them there are. He also knows that they gave him shelter and food and then chose to give him freedom and bring him back home. Far better to work with them, show them our ways and let them see how the land can support us all. I was a stranger in their land and was only shown kindness; mine was a different experience to Epenow. Their ways are different, and I cannot vouch that they are all good people but most are honest and true, and they will be keen to learn about this new land they find themselves in. I think they will be happy to share with us."

"But we have seen too many of them kill for no reason, I don't have your faith, and Epenow's mistrust must have good cause."

"But Massasoit, why start a battle you cannot win? Give me time to show them our ways, and in the meantime, by aligning your tribe with their powerful weapons, you could be strengthening your position amongst all the other coastal tribes."

Passaconaway, the greatest medicine man of our tribe, stands to speak. I hand the talking feather back, and everyone listens to his powerful words.

"I know this arrival means great trouble for our people and for the earth. All the signs are here. There is much to be offended by these intruders arrival. They have defiled our sacred graves, stolen winter corn supplies and fired their peskunck sticks. They seem to take what they want without thinking about their neighbours. This is why we are gathered here now to use our energy wisely, and with all due ceremony, we will now work together to banish the white people from these shores. We will spend three days and nights working on this and then decide the right action. If nothing moves them on then maybe the Creator has intended for them to come here to be taught the ways of Creation."

PLYMOUTH, MASSACHUSETTS, THANKSGIVING 2010

"Can I just stop you there, Gigi?" Sir Ian had been all ears for Grandma's story but wanted to ask a question.

"Am I boring you?"

"No, not at all, and I don't mean to interrupt your flow, it's just that I need to say something while I still remember it. This story started because of that Shakespearean quote from '*The Tempest*,' and I've just thought of another quote from the same play.

"'*When they will not give a doit to relieve a lame beggar, they will lay out ten to see a dead Indian.*'

"What Shakespeare means by this is that the people of London, at least, had already met American Indians brought back by the explorers who had crossed the Atlantic. When Francis Drake was circumnavigating the world,

Shakespeare was still at school in Stratford, which meant he grew up listening to tales of Columbus, Cabot, Frobisher, Hudson and Raleigh - all explorers, who I suppose would have been like the Apollo astronauts of their day. It would have been extraordinary if Shakespeare hadn't been influenced by their astonishing tales of daring-do in distant places. When I've been researching the history of that time for some of my roles, I came across stories about how Native Americans did come to Shakespeare's London, and in fact even earlier in the reign of Elizabeth's grandfather, Henry VII. In one historical account, there were reports of crowds in a plague-ridden London around 1603 being amazed by American 'Virginians' demonstrating their skill in handling their dugout canoe on the River Thames.[10] The sad thing for those early visitors, though, is that most of them had no defence against European germs and they died fairly quickly which is why Shakespeare wrote about them being preserved and put on display."

"Gross!"

I had been sitting quietly listening to Gigi and for the first time realising that actually these are interesting stories and feeling guilty for all those times I just zoned out every time Grandma talked about the past. All those years of her endless research seem to be enthralling our visitor; however, even I felt putting bodies on display a bit much but if Shakespeare wrote it, then it probably happened.

"Well, Taylor, a lot of things about Shakespeare's time were gross: 21st-century noses would find no drains and low public hygiene standards quite a challenge. In fact even an audience with the King, James I, would probably have been a bit of an ordeal. Although he was a very clever Renaissance scholar, he could not help the fact that he had a tongue that was too large for his mouth, so it made him slobber whenever he ate or drank and his personal hygiene was based on an aversion to water that ensured he strictly confined washing to the tips of his fingers.[11] But we do know he was interested in America because Shakespeare's friend, the Earl of Southampton reports in a letter that the King is eager to have one of the Virginia Squirrels that are said to fly. James loved exotic animals, and so I think we can assume he would be just as interested in meeting a genuine Native American.

"Which leads me back to *The Tempest* and the questions Shakespeare is asking in that play. Questions the whole of society were discussing then about the creation of a new society and the boundaries between 'civilization' and 'savagery.' In fact, I'm pretty sure that *The Tempest* is probably the first time in English Theatre that an American Indian character is presented. So you see the years before The Pilgrims arrived here, was an era when Europe was actively encountering 'others' and both London and Plymouth would have been bustling multicultural ports with visitors from many countries. Indian and African servants were not an uncommon sight. So it is highly likely that before Shakespeare wrote *The Tempest*, he may well have encountered a Native American. In fact, the themes of *The Tempest* place the question of what happens when western civilization makes its impact upon other societies before us, in a way we can never forget. Our sympathies are not necessarily with Prospero—and despite his 'savage character' there is something deeply affecting about Caliban and Shakespeare gives him one of his most beautiful speeches. Sorry, I digress, but when you said Squanto lived in England, it just made me think about the ideas inspiring *The Tempest* and how it's so relevant to America."

NEW ZEALAND – FEBRUARY 2012

I can see you've already added a lot of extra details to Gigi's story. I didn't realize that one of the reasons the Pilgrims decided to leave for America was because they saw a comet as God's sign that it was time for them to set up their new world.

SAVANNAH - FEBRUARY 2012

That was how they saw it, but interestingly that comet also coincided with the death of Sir Walter Raleigh, the great guiding star of Elizabethan exploration and cousin to Squanto's sponsor Sir Ferdinando Gorges. The comet was seen in the night sky for nearly two months, so as you can imagine its appearance did cause quite a panic in Europe, enough to convince King James that he should write a poem to tell his people to calm down. The gist of his writing was that even if God had sent the comet, the English were not a race that should go to pieces, *"keep his rash imaginations till he sleep."* I suppose you could say it's an early example of that typical British stiff upper lip attitude.

However, although the King was telling everyone the comet was not something they should worry about, it's intriguing that he decided that this moment should also mark the end of an era for Sir Walter Raleigh. Raleigh's execution was seen as a purely political decision by James to appease the Spanish, but happening as it did in the year of the comet, it marks the sad end of an era for English buccaneers. Interestingly, though, knowing Raleigh is also associated with introducing tobacco to England—one other reason King James may not have been a big fan of Sir Walter—is that he was very much ahead of his time in seeing the problems that smoking creates. He wrote a pamphlet describing it as *"A custome lothsome to the eye, hatefull to the Nose, harmefull to the braine, dangerous to the Lungs."*[12]

What is also amazing to me now is that everything I thought about boring old history has been turned on its head, particularly now I know this is the story of my family. I'm not just borrowing books from the library I'm buying books online and trawling websites and archives for any and every bit of related information I can find. Sherlock Holmes eat your heart out, I am snuffling out evidence anywhere I can find it.

New Zealand, February 2012

Families are fascinating and I had a very interesting chat with Peter Jackson, our director, the other day about his family history. His grandfather fought in World War One and it has made him fanatical about learning everything about that particular period of history just to understand the experiences his grandfather lived through. He also told me something really interesting that he felt might explain his obsession. He read in a magazine, *Discover*, I think it's called, which explains science in everyday language, that new studies on DNA by neurobiologists and geneticists suggest that our DNA may carry the patterns, unconscious memories and traumas from our ancestral line.[13] Imagine that our bloodstreams can still carry the traumas of lifetimes before our own. It's quite a revolutionary idea in science that shows how life experiences could directly affect your genes—and not only your own life experiences, but those of your mother's, grandmother's and beyond. However this sits with you, I think we all sometimes sense an awareness of being bound by ancestral threads, family bonds which came before our conscious self. So maybe everything you are working on was always meant to be. Good luck with your detective work, can't wait to read the next chapter.

SAVANNAH,
FEBRUARY 2012

That is an amazing scientific breakthrough and yet at the same time, seems common sense. It feels like we all know families who seem to share trouble and others who always get the lucky breaks. In many ways finding out about the history of my family has felt more like a rediscovery than something totally new. In so many ways, the more I find out, the more I realise, "Ah, that's why!" rather than total surprise. Well, I've found out a lot more now about what the Pilgrims were doing before they crossed the Atlantic and it really has helped me understand what drove my ancestors to risk everything by sailing to an unknown destination.

Chapter Three

YOU TAUGHT ME LANGUAGE, AND MY PROFIT ON'T, IS, I KNOW HOW TO CURSE

For a Yorkshire farmer's son, a North Sea crossing in a violent gale was not my finest hour. I hadn't realised how seasick I would feel: that, I suppose, and the relief of not being sent to prison again meant I spent most of the journey with my head over the side of the ship. In the end, it was probably a good thing the women and children hadn't escaped with us, as a journey that we were told would only take two days, took fourteen, each one stormier than the last, so that even the sailors had begun to give up hope of reaching safe harbour.[1] But the biggest surprise of all, when we finally reached Holland, was Amsterdam. Austerfield and Scrooby were small country villages that were rooted in the earth and were no preparation at all for living in a city that seemed to grow out of and float on the sea.

At home we walk or ride and know all our neighbours; here everything moves by barge; even the markets are floating, and everyone we pass is a stranger. Everywhere you go, you are surrounded by water, so many islands and bridges, and although the houses seem solid enough the way they grow tall and slender alongside the canals it looks as if they are just waiting for a wind to sail away. You can stand in the north of the city and watch new canals being built, it is as if the city is growing in front of your eyes. This is a port built on trade and the ships that bring in new goods every day In some of the docks, the smells

33

of exotic spices from far-flung places are an assault on the senses. I was used to Yorkshire farmers' markets smelling of nothing but pig and cow dung, but here flowers and spices give everything a more pleasant and perfumed aroma and literally anything is for sale. You can go to the port to see new arrivals and cargo every single day, not least more separatists like ourselves.

The minister of Gainsborough, a congregation just a few miles from Scrooby, has decided that they too will make this tolerant city their new home. That, however, is our problem, our fellow English separatists all have different ideas about how to worship, and we are being asked to get involved in arguments we have no place to judge. Our minister John Robinson has decided in order to quietly establish the way we want to worship, we need to be free to do this on our own terms and in our own way, so the decision has been made, we need to move again. The city of Leiden is to be our next stop, there is a suitable house not far from the Pieterskerk, one of the city's largest churches, and there is a lot of work there in the weaving shops. William Brewster thinks he can teach at the university and it has been decided it will be an excellent place to set up our own printing press. These are exciting times, in a country that allows us to worship as we want.

PLYMOUTH, DEVON, JULY 17TH, 1605 – SQUANTO'S ARRIVAL

This ocean is far bigger than I had ever dreamt of; no canoe would ever make this crossing. The stranger's sails are stationary clouds that catch the wind's breath to push us across the endless water. I have chosen to go and want to learn more about the strangers, but the crew set sail with four other warriors on board. They are from different tribes and have not chosen this journey, so they battle at first, not knowing what the strangers want or how they mean to use us. I am able to reassure them that I have been with the strangers three nights already and they have fed me kindly and appear to want to know as much about us as I want to find out about them. I tell them to trust the ale and peas and share the food to show it is not poisoned. The salted fish is fine, but the meat looks old and grey, so I don't recommend that.

The journey lasts over a full cycle of the moon and in that time we share our languages-we give them our names for the stars, they give us names for their food and show us how the ship sails work to catch the wind. We tell them how we make bread from our corn and milk from our deer. They talk about their "cows" and "pigs" and tell us when we arrive at their home they will give us the finest tasting "bread" in their country.

Whilst we measure time by the sun and moon, the strangers have sand clocks which they use to measure all their work. Eight turns of the clock measures each job; first, they clean the deck, then change the sails and rigging, next turn they pray, then eat, then sleep. Everything set by the movement of sand and the whistle of the man they call boatswain.[2]

After all the endless tossing of waves and turns of the clock, we are now calmly entering one of the most beautiful harbours I've ever seen. Even the Massachusetts tribe would be impressed by this river and its gentle rolling valleys in front of us, and ours wasn't even the biggest boat in the harbour, there are so many ships bobbing and weaving around us. Tahanedo says he will be marking his stick to count how many strangers we came across so we can tell our tribes back home how many more of these white people there are.[3] Already from the look of the crowds around the harbour, I can tell that is going to be a task too far.

I have never seen so many people in one place and so many tall buildings. As we sail by you can see teams of men building, digging into the ground, moving mud and then passing branches between themselves to make yet more buildings that stand two or three trees high so that the paths between them are in shadow. From our perspective on the boat, it is like watching a human anthill busy at work with each person ascribed their own specific job. The energy of so many people in such a confined space is akin to the most powerful powwow you can imagine, there is just so much happening all at once here. It is difficult to know where to look first.

Captain Weymouth anchors the ship and proudly announces he is going to keep his promise and get us that special "bread." It feels odd to get our feet back on dry, steady land, but odder still are the looks of the crowds, and the smells that assail us; all of our senses go into overdrive. Eyes are boring into us from every direction, but it is not a hostile crowd: just an overwhelming feeling of curiosity from us and them. One little boy runs up to touch me. I bend down; I think he wants to see if we are real. I give him a feather, and the crowd laughs as he runs back to his mother hiding his face in her skirts. The captain is on a mission, though, following his nose to the bakery he had told us about. Our moccasins find the stony road lumpy to walk on and at first the smell of rotting food, and unwashed bodies is pretty overwhelming but then we smell it too, a pleasant warm wheaty aroma. The captain is right: this "bread" is something else after a month of dry biscuit. Undoubtedly, there is going to be more to learn about this strange, crowded land than I have ever dreamt of; everything is unlike home, the smells, the sounds, the food, the people, but already we have all laughed together so maybe they aren't as strange as we think, just different.

Bread in hand, Captain Weymouth wastes no time in walking us up the hill to meet the local chief. His fort is impressive, built in a star shape, the walls stand nearly three men high and at least one man deep and boast a view across the whole harbour. We walk through a great stone arch and inside are many warriors with thunder sticks, and I count seven large cannons.[4] Sir Ferdinando Gorges is the first person we meet who tries to speak our language. On the ship, we had exchanged words with the sailors, but this chief has some Roanoke words written on parchment, I am able to roughly translate for the others. He tells us that his cousin another chief, Sir Walter Raleigh, has visited our country and brought back the warrior Manteo from the Croatan tribe in Roanoke. He has learnt some of their language from him, and he tells us that he would like to learn more about us and our land so that more of his people can visit. Nahanada is already muttering that there are far too many of them and that these strangers always seem to want more than they already have.

"Isn't this big house enough for him, why does he want to come to our home? It is not the man who has little but he who desires more that is poor!"

Apparently, it is going to take us all some time to understand the way the stranger's world operates but, as this chief has made such an effort to talk to us, I thought it polite to respond in kind with something the sailors had taught us. "Da durdalathawhy," I respond. This makes both Captain Weymouth and Sir Gorges smile broadly, they are the words we have been taught when offered food, it means "Well, I thank you," but in Cornish, the sailor's language.[5]

NEW ZEALAND.
MARCH 2012

Dear Taylor,

That's some intriguing stuff you've unearthed, well done, you really are turning into a bloodhound and do you know what you've inspired me. The miracles of the Internet never cease to amaze, it's such a wonderful encyclopaedia of information, I've just discovered that the bakery you mentioned is still there. *Lonely Planet* recommends it as "quietly groovy, fantastically friendly and extremely good at baking things." They also say Jacka is one of England's oldest working bakeries (four centuries and counting); as it's meant to have provided the ship's biscuits for the Pilgrim Fathers aboard the *Mayflower*. So it's definitely on our list of places to visit when you come over in the summer.

Meanwhile, keep on sending me your latest material.

SAVANNAH, GEORGIA,
APRIL 2012

Dear Sir Ian,

Sorry for the break, I'd put off my College essays for too long and was going to get into trouble if I didn't deliver. However, I've decided that when I choose my thesis for next year, I may well look at painters of the Stuart Court which will give me an excuse to focus on that period in English history during College hours.

I am finding it easier to write at College than back home. Maybe it's because I've got the distance to be objective about my hometown. No one knows me here,

strangers don't have expectations, they don't judge or at least you can't hear what they think. The only way I can be sure not to get accosted back home is to put my headphones on full blast, a bit of Prodigy usually works; in fact, *"Invaders Must Die"* is always a winner and just gets me running. I was going to say if you come from a small town you'll know what I mean, then I suddenly realised who am I talking to. You must have trouble walking around any town without being stopped! I suppose, I just feel lucky to have survived Plymouth. If all your school years are spent in a hostile environment you get used to cold looks and feeling uncomfortable. I know Gigi told you the story about the boy in my class who took against me. He was the only other pupil who came from a one-parent family, and he chose to see it as a punishment rather than a gift, which is why we clashed. I was proud of my family, he felt only pain and shame. It's a story as old as Adam and Eve. An angry frustrated man blames a woman for all the bad things he is feeling. It escalated over time until one day he brought a gun into school. Thank God he only picked his grandpa's air rifle that day, or we wouldn't be having this conversation. Shooting me was obviously a violent act but actually it was a relief. Violence is not just physical. Every day had been a struggle at school, constantly being belittled, blanked or bullied puts you under stress. After the accident, I became invisible, too obvious a target, so everyone then just gave me a wide berth and I've always tried to keep my head down since. It happened; I'm alive, what doesn't kill you makes you stronger and we move on. As Gigi says, "The soul would have no rainbow if the eyes had no tears." Now I just feel sorry for him. His family confused caring with giving money, it is never equivalent. For a child to feel happy they need a family to lavish then with time, attention and love, nothing else matters. I had the very best start in life, we didn't have wealth but my family taught me the essentials—how to care for others, how to see the bigger picture and how to love. Things, as Gigi would say, can just get in the way.

Savannah has now given me the breathing space I needed from home. To be able to relax and be yourself is such a relief, you suddenly realise how long you have spent being constantly judged. In Plymouth I was a round peg being forced through a square hole. To be considered on an equal footing by your peers is like removing the heaviest boulder you didn't even know you were carrying.

Viewed from a distance, Plymouth is a tiny town with a single-minded obsession about where your family has come from and one particular historic date. It's a neighbourhood in which every person wants to preserve their own version of the past in aspic with a line of white ancestors stepping all the way back on to *The Mayflower*. In Plymouth, there's a belief that this one moment when the Pilgrims stepped ashore changed everything and made America. People travel from all over the states to worship at the "Rock," where our ancestors landed. Who knows if it really is THE "Rock"? That small piece of glacial deposit which was identified as the landing point wasn't chosen until 120 years had passed by and when they moved it to put it in a more public space, it split in two.[6] They put it back together just after the 200th anniversary, and for the 300th it was moved again back to the seashore to give it a more "natural appearance." The truth is that the "natural" appearance of the land as they arrived was that of a holocaust, a plague, unknowingly brought by European sailors but that was so devastating to the locals, it had left the skeletons of Native Americans abandoned with no one left to bury them.

This reverence towards Plymouth as the crucible of America is just crushing. I mean for heaven's sake, before the Pilgrims landed here Leonardo da Vinci had already painted the Mona Lisa, Michelangelo the Sistine Chapel, Galileo had shown the Earth revolved around the Sun and Shakespeare had written all of his plays. There was a lot going on in the world then, but you wouldn't have thought it in my town. No, we revere a four-hundred-year-old cooking pot, a straw hat and a rickety old chair that William Bradford once sat in. Tourists in Rome may stare at the creation of Adam, and we have the threadbare remnants of a Puritan's kitchen.

Apologies for the rant, I suppose my problem is that I've never felt quite at home when at home, there has always been an unease that our family didn't fit in with the usual cliques. A household of unmarried mothers may be more acceptable in New York or London, but we've never blended in. Despite all of Grandma's stories, we were never seen as part of the "*Mayflower*" club. Anyway, I've had a chance to catch up now, so here is my latest work.

PLYMOUTH, MASSACHUSETTS, THANKSGIVING 2010

Watching a cultured European find what Gigi had to say fascinating, made me listen more carefully to what Grandma was saying. Somehow this conversation with Sir Ian felt very different. Maybe I'd deliberately zoned out every time Gigi talked about finding the truth about the past. I just saw it as her obsession and perhaps that's why I'd chosen to study Art History. I wanted to focus on the world before Puritans, see the many glorious visions other's had before my ancestors came along and made work the be-all and end-all.

And Grandma was flattered to have such an educated listener wanting to hear her well-worn story and was even finding the interruptions interesting. But once she started nothing would stop the flow.

"So shall we go back now to William Bradford's deathbed? He's trying to explain to his eldest son John how difficult those early days really were and what an important role Squanto had in helping them survive. In all the official records, as William is such a spiritual man, it is always God's will that helps them through these difficult days, but for John the son he wants to be honest with, he is ready to admit how much one 'native' did to save their lives."

PLYMOUTH, MASSACHUSETTS, 1657 – BRADFORD'S DEATHBED

"We had barely survived the winter, John, death was everywhere our numbers were halved by illness—at one point two or three were dying each day—and as we watched our friends pass away, we also knew that we were being watched. We saw many signs of Indian activity, and none of it looked friendly. Worst of all were the horrible cries from the Powwow the local tribes had called. We were in a strange country, had already been attacked on our first encounter and had heard so many stories about wild savages that we could only expect the worst. I was struck down with fever myself. In fact, whenever the alarm was sounded, we'd be dragged from our sick beds propped against a tree and a gun put in our hands just to look threatening. By the end of winter, we were very easy prey. In fact if they had wanted to, the natives could have put an end to New England before we had even begun. Many wanted to destroy us, which would not have been difficult in our weakened state but despite being a prisoner of the tribe, Squanto was allowed to be part of these noisy discussions and even in his weakened position, such were his powers of persuasion, he was able to convince the majority that with our guns we'd be more useful as allies to keep larger tribes at bay."

PLYMOUTH, MASSACHUSETTS, MARCH 1621 – SQUANTO'S VIEW

Epenow and his tribe were not happy but after days and nights of chanting and deliberation, it was decided, for the moment, that we would talk peace. Passaconaway, our spiritual chief, had listened to everyone's view and then we all, however begrudgingly, agreed a course of action. He had given me the responsibility to show the white people our ways and how to fit in with our culture. I had been given four seasons starting now with the spring equinox.

Patuxet is our sacred space, and before the next Feast of Dreams, Passaconaway wants our tribe to be able to use the old Vision Chairs again. The strangers had stood on them as they arrived and the tribes need to claim them back.

I had been watching the camp and could tell they were weak, but their war chief was not one to mess with. Whilst others had fallen ill, he was continually pacing and getting his warriors to practise using their guns and loading the cannon. Half the size of our tallest warriors, I could see his sword had been shortened so as not to drag on the floor and his red beard reflected the red mist in his eyes when he sensed danger. Like Epenow he was one to attack first, then ask questions. Little Chimney suits the man's style—always ready to blow, and he was the one I had to make peace with first.

Massasoit had already sent in Samoset to test the waters, and he had come back praising the stranger's beer, but now he was willing to trust me to make the peace deal on pain of death, whilst he and all his warriors watch.

We enter the camp unarmed ready to trade, we have fur skins none of which I'd seen in the camp, and as they don't appear to have any fishing nets, I took a few fresh herring.

Everyone in the group stops their labouring and building as we walk in. I head towards their war chief, Little Chimney, who is standing next to the man I take to be their peace chief.

"We come to trade and make peace."

The instant I speak I know they are all surprised at my English, and I can hear them talking amongst themselves, it appears to be in English, but with accents I'm not familiar with.

It is at precisely this moment, way ahead of the time agreed, that Massasoit decides his sixty painted warriors will appear on the hillside overlooking the camp; not a helpful move.

The colour drains from all the faces around me just as the redness rises in Chimney, the group are frightened, and his anger feeds from their fear. As expected he holds a gun to my head. "What does this mean?"

"Action is eloquence."[7]

"I agree, and what those men are telling me is that they are looking for a fight."

He cocks the gun loudly in my ear.

"You have the guns, all they have are arrows, and I come bearing gifts. If you want to appear strong, you need to act the part."

"Let him speak, Standish." The peace chief holds the man of action back for now and lowers his gun.

"You must appoint an ambassador to speak to Massasoit, our chief. He must take gifts, then if happy, our chief will come and talk peace in your camp."

Chimney is still gripping his gun in suppressed anger, but the others confer and appoint a Mr. Edward Winslow to carry gifts. Whilst the peace chief chooses gifts, Chimney gives Winslow armour and a sword. We walk back up the hill to Massasoit and his brother.

The knives, copper, biscuits, and alcohol are all willingly accepted, and the salutation of love and peace from their chief, King James, appears to pacify Massasoit, but he is not keen on walking down into their camp to meet Governor Carver. He wants Winslow's armour. We compromise; I suggest Winslow stays with his brother Quadequina whilst we join the English with twenty of his men but without their bows. An argument begins.

"Why should we go into their camp unarmed and they keep all their 'peskunk'?"

I remind him it's not their guns that he should worry about but their barrels of death. I promise that no harm will come and if anything happens, he knows my life is forfeit.

The English meanwhile prepare, as suggested, a regal reception. Chimney is taking no chances and has half a dozen men armed to greet us, each man marks a warrior, so he has seven warriors as hostage whilst a drummer and trumpeter accompany Massasoit and his chief warrior, Hobbamok with all due ceremony into their half-built hall. Governor Carver offers to kiss Massasoit's hand, and gets a hug in return, which I can tell is a surprise as Carver flinches but the two leaders then calmly sit on a green woollen rug and cushions, and our Sachem is impressed by the seating arrangements. More alcohol is provided, and as the drink takes it effect Massasoit begins to tremble a little, whether it's the first time taste of brandy, fear of guns or the all too intimidating presence of the unstable Chimney breathing down our necks who could tell?[8] Their peace Governor does not appear to be too strong a man and Chimney is ready and armed to take over. The trumpet, however, proves to be the masterstroke in this English ceremony, as it creates a great distraction with Massasoit ensuring all his braves take it in turn to show how hard they can blow and so the peace begins and to prove our friendship, I go to the river and catch eels for the celebration meal.

PLYMOUTH, MASSACHUSETTS, 1657 – BRADFORD'S DEATHBED

"I wasn't Governor during the peace talks then John, just an observer, but the one thing I do remember about that day, is how Massasoit did sweat most profusely. At the time I thought it was the drink but looking back I now think Squanto's stories about us keeping the plague in barrels beneath the storehouse probably made him nervous. Yet if it helped us get a Peace agreement with a leader who could have wiped us out in a stroke then who are we to argue? What Massasoit thought were our plague barrels were actually only our gunpowder barrels and I remember about a year later when we dug up some of the gunpowder kegs, Hobbamock, Massasoit's faithful advisor who had also come to live with us then, asked if we really did, indeed, have the plague at our beck and call. The answer he got was as honest a one as I could give, I told him, 'No, but the God of the English has it in store, and could send it at his pleasure, to the destruction of his or our enemies.'[9]

"Not long after that conversation, Massasoit asked me, 'If you would let out the plague to destroy one of my enemies, I promise that I and all my descendants would be your everlasting friends, so great an opinion I would have of the English.'

"And he did stay faithful to Plymouth for the rest of his life, but his trust in us was not shared by his children …. Do you remember John Billington?"

"You mean the first man to be hanged for murder here?"

"Well, he and his family of strangers were troublemakers from the start, but no, I actually meant his eldest son John and was forgetting you never met, I remember now, he died just before you arrived. It was not long after we had sown our very first crops and we seemed to be making the peace really work. John was a young lad then, and he just went wandering. We thought he'd got lost but looking back now, I realise he was probably deliberately kidnapped.

He went missing for five days in July and then we heard that he was being held by the Nausets in Cape Cod. Unfortunately for us, that was the very tribe that we had fought with on our arrival here, back then we had taken their winter supply of corn, and although we promised ourselves we'd pay them back, with all that happened that winter, we never did. Now we had to go back and deal with our crime, and this was potentially hostile territory. Squanto came with me and a party of ten men as we didn't know what to expect. The first place we landed on Cape Cod the local tribe were friendly but as Squanto was trying to find out more about John an ancient woman turned up. She said she had never seen English men before and wanted to look us in the eye and as soon as she saw us she started crying and burst into tears and this is when I learnt just how very forgiving Squanto had been to work with us. The old woman told us the story of how all three of her sons were kidnapped by an Englishman, and she had never seen them again, but Squanto was able to calmly reassure her to the point that she stopped crying and even broke a small smile."[10]

NAUSET, CAPE COD, JULY 1621 – SQUANTO'S VIEW

The Nauset Segousquaw looked me closely in the eye, and I felt her gaze as if it was my own mother, searching into my soul.

"Do you know what it is to lose those you treasure more than your own life?"

I returned her gaze and answered honestly.

"I am from Patuxet and so no longer have a tribe."

She nodded. "…but I carried three sons, and all of them were taken by that cruel Englishman, and the reason they chose to go is that a Patuxet warrior told my boys it would be safe."

She was talking about Captain Hunt, the commander of the second ship that arrived with John Smith on our voyage of exploration along the coast. My job had been to help name the coves and rivers so that a proper map could be made and when my work was done I was told I would be finally free to return home to my tribe. I knelt in front of her and lowered my head.

"Nitka, forgive me, I am that warrior my name is Tisquantum, but I too was deceived. I had come here with the Englishmen of my own choice and was told after one last trade I would be free to return home. But in place of that final trade, Captain Hunt chose instead to steal our Indian bodies. He locked us in the bottom of his ship, and we did not see daylight again until the moon had waxed and waned and we had crossed the far ocean. We were put in metal chains and put on display for others to buy, but we were lucky. We were saved by the spirit men of that country far across the sea; they took us into their home and showed us how wise men live without the guns and swords of the angry men. That is where your sons are now, and they are all safe and happy in their new home following a spirit path—you would be proud.”

“But how come you came back and they did not choose to come?”

“I only knew a way back because I had been across the sea before and I spoke the language of the white sails, the people who know how to cross the sea and when a visitor came I asked to travel with them to see my old friends. Your sons all chose to stay and worship the creator as the journey on that first ship was not easy, and none of them wanted to feel that close to death again, but they said if I were ever to come back and find you that I must say that they always think of you in their prayers.”

Finally, Nitka smiled.

PLYMOUTH, MASSACHUSETTS, 1657 – BRADFORD’S DEATHBED

“I asked Squanto what he had told her and he said that even though she may not see her sons again he knew they were still alive if thousands of miles away and the reason he knew this is because he too had been captured by that same captain and sold as a slave with her sons in Spain. This is a man enslaved by the English but chose to put his faith in us because of his faith in God. I asked Squanto why this is something he never chose to tell me and he looks at me straight in the eye and says…

“‘I am a feather, for each wind that blows, I let go and trust the universe and God to carry me.’

“He didn’t want to burden us with the sins of others in the past and judged us by our actions in the present, and that gave him his confidence in us.”

PLYMOUTH, MASSACHUSETTS, THANKSGIVING 2010

"Gigi, you've done it again."

"What do you mean? More Shakespeare?"

"'I am a feather for each wind that blows' [11], that's also from *The Winter's Tale*."

"You know this time I'm not going to let you have this one."

"What do you mean?"

"Feathers are a vital part of North American culture; it's not just the Wampanoag tribe but nearly every tribe across the continent that knows that saying, it's just so Indian. I'm sorry, your magpie writer is going to have to give that one back to Squanto. Feathers mean a lot to Native American tribes. A feather isn't just something that falls from a bird, it means much more. The feather symbolizes trust, honour, strength, wisdom, power, freedom and many more things. To be given one is to be hand-picked out of the rest of the men in the tribe—it's like getting a gift from a high official. So I'm going to stand my ground and say your Shakespeare stole an American saying."

"But all these Shakespeare quotes that are part of your story are making me think I really need to study the chronology of the time Squanto was in England and the plays Shakespeare was writing then."[12]

"Let's not forget it wasn't just Squanto, as you said there were other Americans who travelled to England, like Pocahontas and I believe John Smith on his return to England had already reported some of the conversations Chief Powhatan had with the Virginian settlers, which sound very poetic. '*Why will you take by force what you may obtain by love? Why will you destroy us who supply you with food ... You see us unarmed and willing to supply your wants if you come in a friendly manner; not with swords and guns as to invade an enemy.*'[13] Perhaps as we've digressed maybe this is the point that I explain how Squanto came to know English so well.

"In 1621 when he first met The Pilgrims, Squanto was probably the most well-travelled person in America, having been across the Atlantic at least half a dozen times. The East Coast Indians—the Abenakis—people of the first light—had been encountering Europeans for centuries, starting with the Vikings, Italians, French and Spanish and then there were regular summer influxes of West Country fishermen who just came for the cod. Sir Walter Raleigh used to say if those West Country cod ships were lost '*it would be the greatest blow ever given to England.*' [14] By the turn of the 17th Century, European explorers were coming thick and fast in the battle to claim America as their own, and one such man, Captain George Weymouth from Devon, decided or, as he suggests, '*invited*' some Indians to come back with him, some more willingly than others. On his return to Plymouth in the summer of 1605 he presented the Governor of Plymouth Fort - Sir Ferdinando Gorges - with this group of Indians. As a cousin of Walter Raleigh, Gorges was excited by the idea of America. He saw Native Indians as valuable translators to help with the New England colonization he spent decades promoting, so he didn't see these people as slaves or servants but as he wrote in his book (looking up a quote in Gorges' book) '*the means under God...of giving life to all our plantations.*' [15] So if Gorges' diaries are to be believed, he kept Squanto with him on his estate in St. Budeaux in Plymouth and if he himself taught Squanto to be an interpreter, then the English he would have spoken would probably have been a very courtly West Country upper-class English—rather different from the rural Yorkshire of William Bradford. According to Gorges, that summer he sent three of the Americans onto his friend in London, Sir John Popham, who was then the Lord Chief Justice and would preside over the trial of Guy Fawkes. But, interestingly, despite being kept busy by the most high-profile political trial of the century, by the very next spring 1606, Sir Popham and Gorges were so inspired by living with these natives that they managed to persuade the King to give a Royal Assent for further exploration of America with the establishment of the Plymouth company.[16] Having been able to get the backing of the King so quickly, I would have thought it's likely that one or two of these Indians were used to show James what America had to offer because within months of his approval they were sending out ships on expeditions and by 1607 had managed to set up the short-lived Popham colony. In fact, I have Gorges' book somewhere—in which he writes about all this and what he says about his Indian guests ... '*After I had those people some time in my custody, I observed in them an inclination to follow the example of the better sort, and in all their carriages manifest shows of great civility, far from the rudeness of our common people.*' [17] So he was obviously impressed by Squanto and his friends."

"Gigi, sorry to interrupt yet again but would you mind reading me that quote one more time?"

"You mean the one from Sir Gorges? He says, '*I observed in them an inclination to follow the example of the better sort, and in all their carriages manifest shows of great civility, far from the rudeness of our common people.*'"

"Doesn't that sound like *The Tempest* quote to you? '*...more gentle-kind than of our human generation you shall find, many, nay, almost any.*'[18] Look, here's a thought, what if we imagine that Shakespeare had met with Sir Ferdinando Gorges? There are several well-known pubs like The George or The Mermaid just near The Globe, and in fact, Sir Walter Raleigh started a club at The Mermaid and would meet up with friends like Shakespeare, Beaumont, Fletcher, and Donne and share his American tobacco. Although London was one of the biggest cities of its day, with a population of around 200,000, it was much easier for the famous and infamous to meet and share their stories. So you can just imagine in one pub or another, writers getting great inspiration first-hand about the new continent. And if Gorges popped in to talk to one of his sea captains or his cousin, Shakespeare could have overheard him talking about his Native American friends. So maybe that was the inspiration behind Gonzalo's speech in *The Tempest*. Gonzalo wonders aloud to Prospero whether anyone back home would believe his report of the people of the island, who are '*of monstrous shape*' but have manners—'*more gentle-kind than of our human generation you shall find, many, nay, almost any.*' Is he talking about the gentle-mannered Indians of Gorges who show *great civility and follow the example of the better sort*? Mixed with Sir Walter's description of the headless men he described in his writings about his discovery of Guiana? Shakespeare took inspiration from everyone he met and all he read—he was just a great magpie as you say and used anything he came across to create the sparkles in his drama."

"Well, maybe—I'm not the Shakespeare expert. I'm not interested in made-up stories, all I've done is try to find out what actually happened to Squanto. There aren't many facts, but Sir Ferdinando talks about Squanto a number of times and uses this group of Indians he's been given, to help with further explorations. From what I've gleaned he kept Squanto close and it is possible that Squanto was living in England from 1605 until 1614 because the next time we hear directly about Squanto is from the journals of Captain John Smith on his exploratory trip to New England in 1614."

"So for all the research you have done, you are telling me that it is possible Squanto was in England for nearly a decade. But what a decade that would have been, those were the years Shakespeare wrote some of his most famous plays *Othello*, *King Lear*, *Macbeth*, *Antony and Cleopatra*, *Coriolanus*, *The Winter's Tale* and *The Tempest*. You already know now, that the quote on the back of that painting is from *The Tempest* and you have already given me a line from *The Winter's Tale* as a family saying. What if Sir Gorges took Squanto with him to court? What if he had met Shakespeare? This is fascinating."

"Look, Squanto meeting Shakespeare is not a line of research I've ever thought of. I've just focused on finding out the few facts I can on Squanto's travels that are hidden in various letters and journals by English men like John Smith, who are extremely keen to sell their own stories of discovery and hero-ism, but are not big on giving credit to others. However, if you look carefully, you can find Squanto there between the lines, quietly helping, translating and observing. John Smith was a man obsessed with America, and he befriended Sir Gorges in Plymouth in order to fund more explorations. When he talks about his mapping of the New England coast in 1614 that Sir Gorges organ-ised, he talks about travelling with a Tantum, who his good friend Sir Gorges provided as a translator: Tantum being short for Tisquantum, which is Squanto's full name. It is impossible to believe that John Smith could have ne-gotiated the New England coast without local knowledge. He writes long lists of accurate Indian names, describing the local coastline, for example in his diary he talks about travelling: 'Southward along the coast and up the Rivers we found Mecadacut, Segocket, Pemmaquid, Nusconcus, Kenebeck, Sagada-hock, and Aumoughcawgen; And to those Countries belong the people of Se-gotago, Paghhuntanuck, Pocopassum, Taughtanakagnet, Warbigganus, Nassaque, Masherosqueck, Wawrigweck, Moshoquen, Wakcogo, Passhara-nack,' etc. These are not English words, they simply would not have been fam-iliar sounds to a man called John Smith! They are all Indian names and he could never have made such an accurate list without a translator, he must have had an expert on hand which he says was Squanto."[19]

"But anyway, back to Squanto's adventures with The Pilgrims in the brief time he had left."

"Oh dear, Gigi—what a spoiler—I thought the story still had a long way to go?"

"Well, the story does, it's complicated but sadly Squanto's time with Bradford is limited so shall we go back to William's deathbed confession?"

PLYMOUTH, MASSACHUSETTS, 1657 – BRADFORD'S DEATHBED

"We had just got back into the boat ready to sail further up the coast when the Nauset leader Aspinet arrived on the beach with a hundred men many of whom undoubtedly we had fought with on First Encounter beach back in December. Yet again this was another moment where the wrong word could have ended it all: keeping our guns at the ready, we asked Squanto to tell them to approach just two at a time. One of the first to approach was the man whose corn we had stolen, and we promised to make good. Then we saw young John Billington being carried out to the boat by a warrior, none the worse for his adventure, he even had a string of shell beads around his neck. In thanks, we presented their leader with a knife and declared peace, and it felt good to right the wrongs we'd committed during our first few anxious weeks.

"But then we hear very worrying news from Aspinet: he tells us the Narrangassets have kidnapped Massasoit, which - if it were true – meant, according to the terms of our treaty, we were already at war with the biggest tribe in the region and we'd only left a dozen men back in Plymouth. We had to return at once, where we found that Massasoit had only been taken temporarily, but now one of his supposed allies Corbitant was working against him. The peace treaty was looking more and more fragile. Squanto and Hobbamock go to investigate and the very next day an exhausted Hobbamock returns fearing Squanto is dead as when he last saw him one of Corbitant's warriors was holding a knife to his chest. This is the point where though we are men of God and come in peace we needed our military advisor Myles Standish to ensure we could keep the peace. And his decision was to hit quickly and hit hard, there was no time to lose, Standish would lead ten men on a rescue mission, and if Corbitant had killed Squanto, he would get his just reward.[20] They left the next morning with Hobbamock as their guide.[21] They attacked the camp under cover of darkness with all guns blazing only to find that Corbitant had already escaped and Squanto was still alive. Only one man and woman were injured that night and our physician Mr. Fuller was soon able to attend to those injuries. What was interesting, though, is that over the next few weeks just as Standish had predicted the show of force had won us some respect with the local tribes, and a lot more local chiefs wanted to become our friends.

"Squanto was quick to advise using this new power to our advantage, and within a month he had persuaded nine local chiefs to come to Plymouth to sign loyalty to King James including Corbitant, who Squanto wisely convinced us was more useful on side. Canacum who had craftily sent John Billington to the Nausets to show us the weaknesses in Massasoit's claims to power and Epenow who had been up to this point the leader of resistance to our arrival. In one fell swoop, Squanto the canny politician had brought them all into our fold and possibly shown Massasoit's influence to be much weaker than he claimed. I don't really know how he made this miracle of bringing all the tribes around us to make peace but to be honest after all we had gone through we needed God and the Indians on our side. Squanto brought us both and what I do know is not a drop of blood was shed whilst I had his guidance, and without him, so many died. Not only did Squanto bring us peace but perhaps more importantly for the long term he then successfully negotiated the most valuable trading partner for Plymouth with the Massachusetts tribe. It was just a few weeks after the peace talks that we went north to Massachusetts Bay, and there he persuaded a group of three squaws to give us the fur off their backs in exchange for just a few baubles, explaining that back in London that fur makes a princely sum. When all we had been worried about was survival, none of us had thought of such a trade and in the end what Squanto instigated for us became the means by which we were able to pay back all our loans."

PLYMOUTH, MASSACHUSETTS, THANKSGIVING 2010

"Grandma—sorry I'm going to interrupt now but this Epenow—you've mentioned, he's actually on Wikipedia—I've got it here on my phone. It says

Epenow was taken captive from Martha's Vineyard by a Captain Edward Harlow in 1611, he couldn't sell him as a slave to the Spanish, so he became a 'wonder,' a spectacle on constant public display in London. Sir Ferdinando Gorges wrote that when he met him, Epenow 'had learned so much English as to bid those that encountered him "Welcome! Welcome"'!"

Sir Ian eagerly looks at my screen and then adds excitedly, "And wait a minute, Taylor—look what it says here—Epenow is said to be the inspiration for the 'strange Indian' mentioned by Shakespeare in *Henry VIII* who was probably being displayed in a theatre or pub, so we have another link back to the bard. '*What should you do, but knock 'em down by the dozens? Is this Moorfields to muster in? Or have we some strange Indian with the great tool come to court, the women so besiege us?*'[22] Well, that's a particularly 'bawdy' reference by the Bard about his 'tool,' but I think we get his drift. Interestingly just because it is—that play is also responsible for burning down the original Globe, as it was during a performance of *Henry VIII* in 1613, that a cannon shot employed for special effects ignited the theatre's thatched roof and the beams."

"But it also says, Gigi, that Epenow convinced Sir Ferdinando Gorges (him again) that there was gold back in Martha's Vineyard, so he commissioned a voyage in 1614 and as soon as they arrived back Epenow escaped and then became an important source of anti-English resistance when the Plymouth colonists arrived six years later. So we have two Americans who have first-hand experience of the English with completely opposing views. And one Englishman with a Spanish-sounding name from Plymouth, who is constantly funding expeditions to America that never quite achieve their aims."

Gigi tops up Sir Ian's drink while he thinks out loud on our latest discoveries.

"So both Epenow and Squanto had met Sir Gorges. In fact, he was most likely the instigator behind both the voyages of discovery which brought them across the Atlantic to England, but then he is also the sponsor of their voyages back to America. Maybe Epenow is the model for Caliban—he doesn't sound at all happy with the English, you can imagine him thinking that line: '*Damn you for teaching me your language!*'" [23]

SAVANNAH, GEORGIA, APRIL 2012

It's fascinating when you stand back and look at the arrival of *The Mayflower* from the Native American perspective. Despite Epenow's fundamental mistrust of the English, most of the tribes simply saw a small raggle-taggle group of weedy white people who are more of an irritant than a serious problem. Their main concerns at this point were with the other major tribes in the area like the Narragansett, and so for Massasoit, strategically it was simply a matter of survival for the Wampanoag tribe to befriend the visitors. If they could be used to strengthen their arm in local rivalries then it was a useful alliance.

NEW ZEALAND, APRIL 2012

Taylor, you are so right, all the Thanksgiving stories I ever remember being told were about how the Indians were very helpful to the newly arrived Pilgrims. Well, that may be partially true, however, as you say it was much more about political expediency. The Pilgrims could easily have been wiped out, if the Wampanoag tribe had not been so vulnerable. However, having been persuaded that an alliance with the Pilgrims guns would give Massasoit an extra edge when it came to standing up to the Narragansett, it looks like the decision was pragmatic rather than altruistic. The Pilgrims could easily have been yet another failed colony, without the help and guidance from someone who understood the local politics and how fragile a tightrope they had to tread to survive. As you say the locals made a fateful decision to allow the weak white people to settle. Little did they know what it would lead to!

Chapter Four
MORE SINNED AGAINST THAN SINNING

PLYMOUTH, MASSACHUSETTS, AUTUMN 1621 – SQUANTO'S VIEW

It has not been easy teaching the English how to live on our land. It's not that they don't want to work hard, far from it — it's just that they don't know our ways and arrived in such a helpless state. They land in the freezing cold of winter when nothing can be grown, they appear to have no fishing or hunting experience and rather than use a bow and arrow they shoot indiscriminately at wildlife often scaring the game away and losing all chance of a kill. Though some say they have worked the land, they are all to be taught from scratch how to work with our soil and our corn. The peas and barley they brought with them do not like our earth and have withered away pining for their homelands. I have to show them how their "stolen" corn should be grown and even how to catch fish and stomp for eels, none of them appears to have any real-life skills. They say they can make cloth but what good is that if you can't feed yourself? Even when I showed them how to open the shells of the easiest catch of all quahogs and mussels, they reject this good food because it's not what they eat! On any walk down to the beach you can pick up a juicy lobster or crab but again they think for some reason it's shameful to eat such food.[1] They are challenging people to reason with.

And this particular group of English people were unlike others I have met in that they always expect the worst to happen and find it difficult to trust others. The way they focus so much on problems they almost want to ensure unfortunate things happen—or at least Little Chimney does.

Within weeks of the peace deal, their chief Governor Carver collapsed in the fields. I was concerned that Chimney might take over, however, when they gather to decide who the next leader will be, it is just the men of their tribe who make the decision and it appears to me that it is just those with the loudest voices who are heard. However, they make the right decision and chose another spirit man, William Bradford. He has not been well himself but has potential, and over time I have hopes he will understand how our tribes need to celebrate the seasons in our sacred place again. Already as the autumn equinox approaches soon after our crops of corn, squash and beans have been harvested, Bradford has agreed that having gathered in the fruits of our hard labour it was time to rejoice together in a memorable way.

On the chosen day, William decides to dress in his special red waistcoat and suit with silver buttons.[2] He even takes time to trim his beard. This gives me much hope, for the last year these white men have struggled to adapt to our land, they have barely survived away from their own mother soil and taken little care in their appearance. That William takes time to dress as a white Sachem, shows me that he understands the import of this moment. I have to admit he was surprised at the numbers Massasoit brought with him, over a hundred of his tribe, twice the number of English, but they did bring a very welcome five deer, and to that, we added wild turkeys and the ducks and geese who always arrive at this time of year. Spirit master Passaconaway is pleased we are making progress, although Bradford has strongly cautioned that we can't be entertaining this many people all the time.

There was one moment of sheer joy in the celebrations that no one will forget. I do remember the music and songs of London as being some of the most magical sounds I've ever heard, and when the Pilgrims started to sing a song to celebrate the feast I recognised it for a tune I had heard before, but it wasn't just me all the Wampanoag tribe joined in. Later Hobbamock, Massasoit's shaman told me that ever since the plague had attacked our tribe, those who survived dreamt of music and this was the sound, it was the White Man's song.

Plymouth, Massachusetts, Thanksgiving 2010

"Gigi, how on earth do you know that story about the music they all heard?"

"Well, I have read about it in a few dusty archives, and it has long been a story that I have heard from others. 'O Sacred Head, Now Wounded' was a Christian Passion Hymn, which adopted a popular tune by a German composer called Hans Leo Hassler, written around 1600. Certainly, the Pilgrims would have known the hymn as did Bach, who then adopted the melody for his St Matthew's passion and that was the inspiration for Paul Simon when he wrote American Tune."[3]

"American Tune—one of my favourites," and Sir Ian begins to sing:

> *Many's the time I've been mistaken*
> *And many times confused*

Gigi now joins in ….

> *Yes, and often felt forsaken*
> *And certainly misused …………………*
> *Oh but I'm all right, I'm all right*
> *I'm just weary to my bones*
> *Still, you don't expect to be*
> *Bright and bon vivant*
> *So far away from home, so far away from home.*

They both laugh.

"What are we like?"

"But do you remember the last verse?"

Sir Ian talks it out:

> *We come on the ship they call the Mayflower*
> *We come on the ship that sailed the moon*
> *We come in the age's most uncertain hour*
> *and sing an American tune.*

And in my head, despite Gigi's awful singing with Sir Ian, I suddenly felt goosebumps to be thinking that this was a tune that all the Indians heard in their heads before *The Mayflower* arrived and they and the Pilgrims sang it together at that very first Thanksgiving.

Sir Ian beams, "Well, isn't that just the wonder of music and melody in crossing time and culture and bringing people together? '*Such sweet thunder.*'" [4]

PLYMOUTH, MASSACHUSETTS, WINTER 1621 – SQUANTO'S VIEW

But I am concerned that the peace is still fragile. Massasoit is clearly enjoying the strength aligning with the English is giving his tribe and he is acting with ever more arrogance which has not gone unnoticed by the Narragansett's to the north. Their chief Canonicus is getting disturbed and may cause us trouble. Although more young English men have recently arrived, again it is at the wrong time of year, after the harvest, so although there is more strength in numbers, there are not enough supplies to ensure these people have any strength to survive.

Two weeks before the winter solstice the Narragansett Sachem decides to send us a threat brought to us by one of his tallest and strongest young warriors. Walking proudly into our camp, he lays a bundle of arrows wrapped in a rattlesnake skin directly at Bradford's feet. No matter what I say about this "gift," there is no likelihood that Chimney doesn't recognise the imagery for what it is. This is no peace talk, and the Narragansetts have enough warriors to overrun the camp in an instant. We have to be bold. I tell Bradford to respond with the strongest message we can. This is "*when the battle's lost and won.*"[5] We know this tribe has five thousand warriors standing by who could easily crush us. William has to understand how important the theatre of threat is. This is the moment and William plays his role perfectly. With great ceremony, confidence and deliberation: in front of this angry warrior he fills the wrap with gunpowder and lead round shot and hands the now poisoned snakeskin back directly. Miantonomi couldn't have made a more worried exit as he gingerly holds the parcel that he clearly feels could explode any minute. [6]

But now there was no chance for a peaceful celebration at winter's onset. Chimney was swept away into battle mode, and on his orders, they start to build a high wall of wood around the entire settlement. [7] This means the English sacrifice hundreds of trees to his plan – a town of dead trees, laboriously chopped down and dragged from the forest by men weakened on rations that can only feed half their number – this is not going well.

With such lack of trust to other tribes around us, I knew that Bradford and Chimney would not countenance a visit by anyone, even from our tribe around the winter solstice. What I didn't imagine is that they would not even let their own people celebrate the shortest days. The new arrivals refuse to work on their Christmas Day which Bradford agrees with, and he lets them rest, whilst he and the older settlers go out to work. However, when they come back at midday, he is angry to find that they are playing games in the street. Bradford angrily confiscates all their balls and bats insisting that it is not fair that some play while others work, they can have their Christmas at home but no gaming. [8] These people are all work and do not feel the need to balance their day with enough rest and repair. Tension is building within and without the settlement. For the sake of the English and the Wampanoag, I may well have to talk politics with the Narragansett if we are to maintain this fragile peace.

Just like my "kidnap" was able to secure the loyalty of all the local tribes to the English for fear of their bloody retribution, perhaps a plan to show the English how Massasoit is a potential danger to peace in the whole region is needed? I will have to talk to others and soon.

NEW ZEALAND - MAY 2012

Taylor, I know the Puritans were quite strict but is that really true about Bradford not even allowing a bit of fun on Christmas Day?

SAVANNAH - MAY 2012

Well, I was surprised too but I've cross-checked the story from several sources and even William himself wrote about how he objected to them

playing games, which was an English tradition. The newcomers were used to celebrating Christmas this way but that was not what the Puritans did, and William was making it clear that it was their rules in New England no matter what happened back home. He was ensuring that they were creating a new God-ordained nation and it was the strictest Puritan rules that everyone was expected to obey.

PLYMOUTH, MASSACHUSETTS, 1657 — BRADFORD'S DEATHBED

"John, we spent all that second winter building a fortress. In many ways, our town now looked like the shape of the ship we had sailed across in, but unlike the *Mayflower*, with its sails, we knew this was a town that wasn't going anywhere. We wanted to show the Indians that we were here to stay and Miles Standish worked all winter on defence tactics. The men were divided into four groups. There was a plan for what do in the case of fire, and what to do if he was away from the settlement and each man knew exactly what their role was in case of an attack. But at this point in early spring, the peace still looked strong and it was time to start trading with other tribes to get the furs that our group needed to send back home. Then Massasoit's trusted assistant Hobbamock brought us difficult news. He told us that the Massachusetts tribe had joined in league with the Narragansetts and were planning to attack Standish as he led our trading party. With Standish out of the way, they would then attack us. Worse still Hobbamock said that Squanto was in on this plot and all winter whilst we had been working on our wall he had been secretly meeting with leaders throughout the region.

But we were running out of food yet again and had to start trading. I had spent all this last year in the close company of Squanto and could not believe he would betray us and Standish had an equally close relationship with Hobbamock and felt that he too was a man to trust. It was decided that we just had to forge ahead—starving wasn't going to help anyone, and we had to trust that Hobbamock had misread Squanto's intentions. So in April Standish set off with both Squanto and Hobbamock for Massachusetts but a few hours later an Indian who we were told was a distant relative of Squanto appeared outside the gates with a bloody face, shouting that Massasoit had teamed up with the Narragansetts for an assault on Plymouth.

What concerned me most is that this was a suspiciously similar ruse to Hobbamock's escape from Corbitant last year; I decided to immediately fire the cannons as a warning signal knowing that it was probably too late to recall Standish but wanted anyone working outside to have a chance to return to the safety of the town. As it turns out Standish did hear the cannon and turned back. Immediately on arrival Hobbamock angrily insisted that the claims of Squanto's relatives were all lies, as he would know if Massasoit was planning anything. So to see what truth there might be to the story, it was decided to send Hobbamock's wife back to Massasoit's village.[9]

The message Hobbamock's wife brought back from Massasoit was that he was totally loyal to the peace treaty and would always warn of any possible threats should they arise.

But over the next few weeks, Standish was to insist that Hobbamock's view that Squanto was trying to overthrow Massasoit to get power for himself was the only reason behind his behaviour. Squanto must have hoped that the false alarm might have prompted us to attack Massasoit. I couldn't or wouldn't believe this of Squanto—everything he did was to help us as a community and how could I be sure this wasn't a plan by Massasoit to besmirch Squanto's reputation?

PLYMOUTH, MASSACHUSETTS, MAY 1622 – SQUANTO'S VIEW

"The traitor must die."

I was impressed that Hobbamock's translating skills had improved so quickly now that he was living alongside Little Chimney.

Both Massasoit's messengers were pointing at me. Bradford looked confused, Chimney knew precisely what was happening, but it was left to me to translate the detail. They were holding the tribal execution knife belonging to Massasoit and clearly had been instructed to return to camp with my head and hands in exchange for some furs. Bradford was shocked and insisted that my role was vital to the welfare of the camp; however, this was not a decision that was going to go away. My life was in his hands, and it wasn't for me to make excuses to my executioners. I was not sure which was more important to Bradford at this point, the need to keep the peace with Massasoit or our friendship. We had grown close, and it was because of our spiritual understanding that I had decided to talk to the Narragansett to ensure peace for the English was spread over a far larger area. However, until the plan had a chance to work, I had not discussed the detail with anyone, and Hobbamock simply translated it as the breaking of our peace treaty. I could tell Bradford was tormented and then a ship appeared on the horizon, and he quickly decided that until he knew if it was a threat or not my assistance was still required.

The ship was not good news. Sixty more settlers who were looking to be fed, including young men who are so hungry they eat green cornstalks ruining the crop for everyone else. These people just don't know how to work for the good of the group, and they also bring further tricky news. After Powhatan of Jamestown had died, his successor, Opechancanough was far more resentful of the English ways. His patience had snapped with the ungratefulness of his English guests, and on one day his tribe, feigning friendliness, entered the towns and killed all the men, women and children.[10] I can understand how a misunderstanding of English ways can easily lead to all sorts of problems but now my ideas of peaceful collaboration in the North are not looking hopeful when these settlers believe the worst is just around the corner and are focused on only that as a potential outcome. Bradford is now convinced like Chimney that their big wall is not enough and they need to build a fort. So they now waste yet more time and energy building yet another hostile structure on top of the hill as a threat to everyone around. More killing of trees for men on starvation supplies. The question is how much time, and effort should be put into working on a defence that may never be needed or can never be enough against the might of a greater tribe? For Chimney threats are all around, and no one is to be trusted, and yet the biggest threat to these people is from their own shortcomings. They are surrounded by fertile land and plenty of fish and game, and yet they spend all their time building forts and wonder why it's so difficult to feed themselves?

PLYMOUTH, MASSACHUSETTS - BRADFORD'S DEATHBED, 1657

"With the benefit of hindsight, I now know that Massasoit must have felt threatened and ill at ease by how much I relied on Squanto and referred to him on all major decisions. What I thought was our incredible good fortune to be blessed by God with an expert who had a perfect knowledge of English and local dialects was to become our weakness. He was our only mouthpiece, and the only translator who was bringing all the tribes together or at least forcing them into peace for trade which Massasoit must have felt was weakening his own leadership position. I know that he told Hobbamock to stick with Myles to learn more English and then he used everything he could to persuade us that Squanto was working against us. Finally, Massasoit demands a confrontation meeting with Standish and Hobbamock at which he places his accusations and demands that according to the terms of the peace treaty Squanto must be put to death. He has two warriors standing by with knives, but I cannot believe this of loyal Squanto. However, frustratingly Squanto refuses to defend himself, and simply says stoically, in that Indian way, *what's done is done*,'[11] and asks me to be his judge. I cannot bear to lose my friend, but luckily the arrival of an unexpected ship is a great excuse to put the decision off. I tell Massasoit's warriors we have more pressing concerns to protect our settlement."

PLYMOUTH, MASSACHUSETTS, THANKSGIVING 2010

"Gigi, I'm going to interrupt you again here—you've just given me another quote."

"Really, that other William?"

"Yes, *'what's done is done'* is from *Macbeth*, a play that deals with the issue of betrayal, so I would say Squanto is using this very explicitly perhaps to warn Bradford, but being a Pilgrim I don't think he understands the nuances of what Squanto meant. *Macbeth* was one of the first plays written specifically by Shakespeare for James I because it is about Scotland and witchcraft, one of the King's obsessions."

"But Gigi, how do you know this is what was actually said if it's not been written down?"

"How did people pass on stories for centuries before books? Simply through storytelling, this is the story I've been told, and my mother and her mother before me and poetic words are always the easiest to remember."

And as I'm listening I realise those are exactly the words both mother and Grandmother used when they saw me in hospital after the shooting.

MANAMOYIK, CAPE COD, NOVEMBER 1622 – SQUANTO'S VIEW

I had not left the camp since May as Bradford did not want me to leave his side and he thought that Massasoit's men would be waiting for me, which was correct. However, with Little Chimney ill, and provisions at an all-time low, it was decided that I should travel with Bradford on a trading voyage to the south of Cape Cod across the bay. The route takes us back across the same shoals that Bradford says almost wrecked *The Mayflower* on their arrival and despite my assurances that I had sailed across them safely twice with Captain Thomas Dermer and a Frenchman, Bradford was gripped by the same sense of tragedy that these people always cling to. I know these English are always talking about God's will be done, so surely if God wills it, we will be safe. However, on this occasion, we agreed to head for shore in a calm bay near the Manamoyick tribe.

As is the custom when white men want to trade, I know the locals will want to hide most of their provisions, and it will take a few days of talks before we can be sure of anything. Bradford, in that typical impatient English way, is most distraught that we can't swap goods within hours of meeting, but after a few nights in their wigwams, their trust is such that we can secure a reasonable supply of corn and beans. Bradford is relieved to the point he is so comfortable he even shares the Manamoyick's tobacco with some of his English drink.

This is the first time I have seen him relax since our celebrations last autumn. We talk about our times travelling far from home, and I can tell he is surprised and intrigued by some of the stories I tell him.

"That was a good meal tonight, food is always tastier when you are hungry, but there are some flavours I have never forgotten from my travels. Have you ever had lamb stew or oranges?"

"You're asking a farmer's son if he ever had lamb stew, plenty! I suppose if you don't have sheep here then that is probably an exotic treat. But oranges, I never saw one in Yorkshire, in fact, I don't think I even knew they existed until we arrived in Holland when I was seventeen but then I've never seen strawberries or gooseberries as big as they seem to grow here. You have the most enormous juiciest wild fruit ever."[12]

"But then my people don't know about mince pies."

"Now you're talking something special, melt-in-the-mouth pastry, that's a festive treat for once a year, but that's made out of dried fruit, whilst here you have so many different berries in every month there is no need for drying. In fact, Squanto, I have to tell you everything about this country is bigger and wilder than at home. Here your forests go on forever and are full of bears and wolves and eagles. At home, our woods are much smaller and our wild creatures are foxes, badgers and rooks. "

"That is true when I visited your land, it does seem to have got rid of any wilderness, your people have tamed Nature's wild edges with fences and fields to feel more in control. We know we aren't, so we simply follow nature's timetable and move with the seasons to follow the food. You stay put in stone houses and get food to come to you and collect many objects to decorate your homes. We only keep what we can carry."

"But then, Squanto, you live in a land of plenty, which has introduced us to so many new creatures and so many different tastes, your pohpukun (pumpkin) is delicious and there are so many fish in the rivers, in spring we could walk on their backs to cross the streams, we have never seen numbers like that before and the Lord knows how my feet are ever grateful for your mahkus (moccasin). If you told me your land was home to unicorns, I would not be surprised. We have learnt so much from each other, the most important lesson of all being never get too close to a Sukuk!" (skunk)

Both Squanto and William laugh: the Englishman has shared a joke and they finally relax after all the tension of the last year.

"You know, William, when I worked in London before I set off on my journey back here, I heard about your group."

"How so?"

"I was working for John Slany of the Merchant Taylor's company in Corn-hill, he also ran the Newfoundland Company, and it was to his office that your request for the use of their *Mayflower* ship came.[13] I was with his company in the hope of being sent back home, and so any requests for trips to America were of great interest to me, and I was always looking for ways to encourage the company to head west so I could return. As it happened my ship arrived earlier, but I was not surprised when you landed."

"Squanto, you are probably more familiar with the ways of London and its business than any in our party, we are all mostly from the North of our country and have spent much more time in Holland over the last thirteen years than we have back home. England is not a welcoming place for us anymore, and we had to leave our homeland so that we could find a land where we can celebrate our God in the way that we want to. Not the way that our King tells us we have to."

"Well, I am glad that you feel this land gives you that freedom, William, and it pleases me to see you so relaxed and happy. It's been so long—not since our autumn festival last year."

"There has been so much to worry about here, but you are right tonight I have let those cares go, and for so many reasons being alongside you is re-assuring. You make me feel that this is now our true home and you give me the confidence that we are doing God's work together."

"I think you are right. When I was born, I had a twin brother who only took one breath and my mother always used to say to me, that I would meet his spirit again someday and I think I have. Truth does not happen, it just is. You and I have both been looking for something more all our lives, I travelled to your land because of that, and you travelled to mine, and finally, we have met the spirit we were meant to meet. I recognize that restless searching soul in you, but surely there must have been some moments of peace and happiness on your journey?"

"There have been moments when I felt I touched the truth I was looking for. I think some of my happiest days were in Holland. We had left the dangers of being imprisoned back in England and we were setting up our community and church just the way our group wanted to worship. They were hardwork-ing, but peaceable times and there was one special place there where I could always found solitude and calm. It was a garden that a professor at the University in Leiden had created. This learned gentleman was a great collector of exotic plants and he had planted flowers and fruits there from all over the world. I believe this man had collected seeds from many sea captains including our own great traveller Sir Francis Drake. Drake's crew had given him cocoa beans from Peru, breadfruit from the Spice Islands and papyrus from Java. And this garden even had its own cabinet of curiosities which had all manner of strange objects I had never seen before, creatures like the crocodile and swordfish, a flying fox and a bezoar stone which I believe Drake himself gave Professor Clusius.[14] It was looking at all these wondrous creations that helped to persuade me that there would be other lands we could live in, and God would provide. You see having grown up in the countryside on a farm, I found living in the city very oppressing, too many crowds, too many people, not enough space to sit and think. We needed and wanted more land and space to start again but whilst we were working in our dark, crowded workshops, this garden was my chance to breathe, smell the beautiful perfumes of exotic flowers and feel close to God and all his creation. What about you, Squanto?"

"There are many special places here that make me feel close to God and just being back in my own land reminds me of my family, of loved ones and kinder, happier days. Yes, just being back in Patuxet again has settled my spirit. Wisdom sits in places, and there is one special place I remember from your country where I felt there to was magic. Did you ever attend the big circle in Southwark?"

"Can you describe it, Squanto?"

"Well, I understand what you mean about cities being noisy, crowded places, without the space we have here to be quiet and think. However, they also have incredible energy, driven by all those minds together in one place, like a field of inspiration that can change the way people behave. With so many thrown together in such a limited space, everyone begins to act like ants or bees, working for the hive, and each person becomes a specialist. They are places where people can be encouraged to find their singular skill. And it was in the big wooden O that I met one of your English spirit men. His special job was just to 'talk story,' and he told tales that inspire and describe just what it means to be human. He too was a William, which must be a name reserved for Great Spirits in your language. The building itself was a circle topped with dried rushes, and from the outside, it looked white and shone like a beacon to attract people in. Once inside the crowds stood thronged together with so much energy just waiting to be directed. It was like a temple of togetherness, in a world of strangers, it was a place to gather, like our powwows and just all feel human even if we didn't understand each other's ways. Then the music would start, '*such sweet thunder*,'[15] the sound of pipes, trumpets and drums beating with the rhythm of a human heartbeat and then words spoken in such a way to make your heart beat faster. Even though I stood surrounded by noise and people, and didn't catch all the meaning of these magic sounds, I was able to see and hear a story of truth and destiny that made me feel part of something bigger, it gave me a sense of belonging to the crowd that made me feel my soul."

"Squanto, I believe you are talking about the London theatre. These are not places I or any of our company would attend, as we believe they can inspire man's baser instincts and to be close to God we need to avoid temptation. The risk of corruption when watching players act in direct defiance of the Scriptures by dressing up as women, acting adulterously or speaking slander is not one we would risk."[16]

"But William, isn't that part of our journey here on this earth? To be with temptation and move beyond? The Holy Brothers in Spain told me about Jesus spending forty days and nights in the wilderness to overcome temptation."

"He did, but then, Squanto, maybe most of us are not as strong as him, and we need to remove our souls from temptation so as not to fall."

"But is it also not true that we find what we are looking for?"

"What do you mean, Squanto?"

"You are a spirit man, and you came here to create a special place to celebrate God, and you found that special place and you are busy creating a community that can praise God in your way. That's what you are looking for. But you brought with you a man who looks for trouble."

"Who?"

"Standish, your man of war—he looks for and finds trouble all around him."

"But Squanto, we were not to know when we arrived if any of your tribes would be friendly. All the reports we had heard showed that they were very likely going to be a threat and all that first winter we heard nothing but warlike cries."

"That was our tribal powwow, and you are right, many wanted you dead, but we talked and talked until the tribes agreed that maybe a peace treaty would work."

"So you were talking all that time to stop others fighting us?"

"I did because I knew why you were here. And in our tribes a chief can only make a decision when everyone has had their say, a Sachem can persuade and influence, but in the end, everyone has to agree, or if they don't, they agree to abide by the majority voice. No Sachem can lay down the law on his own without the tribe being involved."

"Thank you, Squanto."

"No thanks required."

"But they are because I know you had a bad experience with an Englishman and yet you argued our case."

"The man who took me as a slave did not see me as human, but you, Sir Ferdinando and many others did and I judge as I find."

"Why did you never talk about that?"

"You do not need to be burdened about the misfortunes that have come my way. If I am angry or sad, it is not fair to afflict others with my troubles. I would be ashamed to weigh others down with something only I have been chosen to carry."

A silence falls between them which Bradford breaks.

"Both of us sit here alone in our communities, and it is difficult to always have the responsibility for the group on your shoulders, to the point where you forget your own life."

Another pause.

"And then there was the happy day my son was born."

"You have a son?"

"He is back in Holland."

"With your wife?"

"No, his grandparents. My wife came with me but died just after we arrived."

"And you never told me about that."

Instinctively Squanto embraces William as if he is helping to share the burden on his shoulders.

"Say no more, William; I can hear the pain in your heart. You will always miss her, but she will always be with you in your son."

"And I will bring him here but only when it's safe."

Another pause as they drink.

"William, I still have family too."

"But I thought all of your family and tribe had died at Patuxet?"

"They have because it would be unsafe for Ouigina to recognise me as her brother, it could put her life in danger."

"Ouigina?"

"Yes, Hobbamock's wife is my little sister. She was only young when I left on my travels, and she must have like me moved away from Patuxet before the great plague fell."

"But Squanto, Ouigina was the witness that Hobbamock sent to Massasoit to prove your betrayal!"

"And she did the right thing because I had promised Massasoit and our great Spirit master Passaconaway that I would teach you our ways and that we as a tribe would still be able to celebrate the seasons in our special place and I failed."

"What do you mean your special place?"

"Those large stones you see around Plymouth—those are our tribal places to thank God at the passing of the seasons. It was no coincidence that the peace treaty was conducted at the spring solstice as this is one of the special times of year our tribes would celebrate and Passaconaway thought it the auspicious moment to talk peace with you."

"But Squanto, you told me that you learned about Jesus and the one true God on your travels."

"I have, William. It was Sir Ferdinando who first took me to your Christian God in a building full of coloured glass that sparkled when the sun shone on it. And then in Spain when the holy men rescued us from the slave market they showed me how they celebrate your Jesus with beautiful deep and sacred music from the heart. And though we may call him by a different name in this land—there is only one spirit that created this world, and it is good to give thanks to God at the passing of every season. And you have been chosen by God to lead your people but lead them in a different way for a different land—we saw the sign when you first arrived here."

"What do you mean—a sign?"

"We were watching you from the moment your ship arrived. We saw you caught in our deer trap when it lifted you upside down in the tree." [17]

"You saw that?"

"Yes, it made your friends laugh, but to us, it was a sign that you are the one chosen to look at this new world afresh and start again. It gave you an opportunity if only fleetingly to observe the earth from the air like a bird, so when you were picked as the new leader it was no surprise to me.[18] But now I have to ask you to promise me something. The peace between our people is precious and fragile, either side may break it, but it will not last at all if you put too much power into one Sachem's hands. You need to talk to other leaders, not just Massasoit and expand the treaty to include all the big northern tribes. Massasoit will feel threatened but it's essential for long-lasting peace and we haven't got long now."

"What do you mean?"

"I mean, I haven't got long. Massasoit's men have been here—I tasted the bitter weed after we finished eating and in the morning I will be bleeding from the nose."

"They've poisoned you? We must haste back to Plymouth, and Surgeon Fuller will attend to you."

"Nothing can be done for my body now, but before my spirit leaves me, I need you to be a true brother and take me home to my spirit stone so I can give you a gift before I leave."

"Squanto, I will not let you go."

"William, my spirit will always be with you, as it has from the moment we were born and I want you to pray for me, so that I may go to the Englishman's God in heaven. I have loved your country and gentlefolk almost as much as my own and Epenow would say more than my own. I will leave you all my worldly goods such as they are, but you will promise me that when the time is right, and it is safe to do so, you will ensure Ouigina or her eldest daughter get the picture I will give you which comes from your London."

Chapter Five

O Brave New World
that Has Such People In't

Taylor, that is a lot of new information and research to take in all at once! You have been working hard and I love Squanto's description of theatre—"a temple of togetherness." That is just how I feel about the work I have been so lucky to have all my life. I can't think of a better description of those very first theatres which shaped and transformed our culture all those years ago. They are places to gather and share our common humanity, our worst and finest traits and where the lonely can feel a sense of belonging to the group. For me, the word "Theatre" represents all that is best in life. To me Theatre represents a Temple of **H**appiness, **E**xcitement, **A**nticipation, **T**riumph, **R**espite and **E**xcellence. I have always thought of them as magical gathering places, no matter what the entertainment and I will never tire of that relationship between performer and each unique audience that only happens at that moment, in that hour, on that day, in that place; irreplaceable, experiences and memories and how lucky I am to have had so many. But how on earth have you found out all that extra detail?

SAVANNAH,
JUNE 2012

Well, there's been a fair share of discussions with Gigi, who I am ashamed to admit I had never really listened to properly before her conversation with you. Also for the first time ever I'm getting a lot of mileage out of the College library. Used to barely visit it but now I'm on first-name terms with the librarians! Sadly I can't change the facts about what happened to Squanto, and we know he died just two years after the Pilgrims arrived. However, it's difficult to find absolute certainty about the detail of events because you have to read between the lines. I mean the very word HIS – STORY, tells you how we learn about the past. Various men write their version of what they believe or want to be the truth and then you have to check with known facts and read between their prejudices. Decision makers often feel uncomfortable when faced with the unfamiliar, so they may well ignore a perspective they don't understand because it's easier to overlook. There's a Native American proverb Gigi told me that says *"Those who tell the stories rule the world"* and the written stories of that time come from William Bradford's own book which was written a decade after these events actually happened, but it's possible to cross-check the detail with other Pilgrim's accounts and their letters home over the first few years. [1]

Then there are the Native American stories from the time, which are more difficult to prove because there wasn't yet a written history, but Gigi, who has spent her life studying the history and learning the native language, tells me that, at the time the Pilgrims arrived, there were sixty-nine tribes of the Wampanoag nation, so that we really should think of Massasoit as the President of his nation. Massasoit is not his name, it is his title as chief. Many writers have misrepresented Indian culture, translating names like Hobbamock as the devil when in fact it means "one who is humble." Some pretend to be historians and interpret what William Bradford wrote as facts when it was written years after the events and coloured by his own deeply religious views on life.

There are a number of early missionary translations of the Indian language which give you a lot of clues as to what the Indians thought and how friendly relations were in those early days. The Wampanoag way was to always listen to as many different points of view as possible and learn as much as possible from whoever, which included the English. So they listened to these newcomers to see what might be of value from them. One native was totally shocked to be told to hit her children to make them obey by a new immigrant, because in tribal life, child cruelty was unthinkable. Also tribes had many female leaders and some of the early missionaries were soon persuaded that their own women should have more rights. In fact, many of these early missionaries looked at the behaviour of the Wampanoag tribe and questioned themselves as to who was more Christ-like in behaviour between the Natives and the new arrivals.

At the time of the Pilgrims arrival, there were hundreds of stone rows, vision chairs, stone mounds, underground chambers, and standing boulders that marked sacred sites—places for vision quests, astronomical calculations, and ritual ceremonies around the seasons. Near Plymouth, there are at least three known donation boulders, called sacrifice rocks, on which branches were piled as donations, along the Old Sandwich Road south of New Plymouth opposite Telegraph Hill and Morey's Hole. In the region of Manomet Hill, there are large marked boulders, traditionally Indian sacred places that signal alignments to solstice solar horizon events.[2] Gigi has told me she will show them to you when you are next in Plymouth. These places could be described as active memorials were the next generation are asked to make their own sacrifice to remember the actions of the past. They are places where someone might have given their life or given away something so precious that they almost can't live without but they did it for the good of the tribe and so these are places where you are asked to remember that sacrifice by leaving something you can almost not live without. They are about keeping alive the memory and celebrating the lives and sacrifices of ancestors.

What William Bradford learnt through his friendship with Squanto was that Indian laws were strictly consensual: everyone had to agree to them. Tribal life insisted on personal freedom—legitimate authority derived only from the active and free agreement of every person. Other leaders would not necessarily "obey" their Massasoit. Tribes had spokesmen like Massasoit to express their considered views, but such leaders were not comparable to English political officials whose word was law. Indian Sachems had to persuade, cajole and mould public opinion. They could not and did not "govern." So political persuasion was an Indian art form which Squanto clearly relished and his years in Europe had only sharpened his skills. So the days and nights of discussion the Pilgrims heard that first winter and thought were angry war cries were in fact part of a proper democratic decision-making process.

And Squanto's reticence to share the story of his enslavement with William is all part of that same Indian culture: *"It is considered shameful to show anger or impatience for the insults or misfortunes that come your way."*[3] Magnanimity and generosity were what guided Indian behaviour and strict self-restraint minimized confrontations and ensured cooperation. Individuals rarely expressed anger openly; so Epenow's outbursts would have been shocking and showed just how worried he was about what he saw as the invasion of his country. It also meant the tribes would have been very wary of someone like Myles Standish who always appeared on the edge of an explosion but also carried a very dangerous gun! Self-control was simply a central part of the culture. Emotional reserve tempered every facet of Indian life, it was important you didn't burden others with your cares. An individual not only controlled their own anger but suppressed open criticism of others to avoid arousing their anger. It was all about controlling selfish impulses and complying with the demands of others, and Squanto's years in a Spanish monastery would only have amplified all those tendencies, although who knows what William felt about his friend being taught Catholic ways?

It was really only personal relations between the individuals in our story that bridge the differences between these opposed styles of behaviour, which is why the direct friendships between William and Squanto, Hobbamock and Standish were essential for securing those early years of peace.

But of course the rule of law wasn't actually the Pilgrims first concern in those difficult early days; it was simply survival. Before they met and conversed properly with the Indians through Squanto, their view of the local population would have been heavily influenced by traveller's stories of "savages" and "cannibals." However, even John Smith, who talked about savages, wrote in his book about New England that it was easy to trade with the Indians in this area as they were very friendly and welcoming.[4]

So once the pilgrims had created their own friendships they soon understood that these people weren't "*savages.*" They may be "*heathens*" as they hadn't yet found the Christian God, but the Pilgrims were lucky enough to arrive in the midst of an agricultural people, who were farmers and fishermen, who lived in balance with nature; a society with male and female leaders, and a democratic political system. And the Pilgrims letters home tell a story of how friendly the Indians they have made peace with are "*very trusty, quick of apprehension, ripe-witted, 'just' and 'very faithful' in their covenant of peace with us. Very loving and ready to pleasure us …and we ….walk as peacefully and safely in the woods as in the highways of England. We entertain them familiarly in our houses and they as friendly bestowing their venison on us.*"[5]

But the one thing all the new immigrants witnessed was that tribal rivalries were long-lasting and historic and in the end, the Puritans, who began to move into Massachusetts Bay en masse by 1630, decided to use these divisions for their own ends to secure trade and land for their own people at the expense of the locals. So here is my next draft of what happened after Squanto.

PLYMOUTH, MASSACHUSETTS, 1657 - BRADFORD'S DEATHBED

"Understanding between two cultures is what Squanto gave us, John. I didn't really understand just what a treasure he was until he was gone and I need you to understand that was true of both you and your mother. John, if God is punishing me, or teaching me to treasure what I have whilst I have it, then I take the lesson to heart. You are precious, John, and I miss you—it's been seven years."

"Then why did you send me away?"

"You know why."

"Yes, you just thought it was time for me to marry a good Christian girl and move on."

"There's more to it."

William coughs; this is clearly a struggle for him now.

"But I need to press on, first I need you to hear all my confession. That second winter without Squanto was really tough, but this time it felt even more dangerous. We now knew about the Jamestown Massacre. 347 English colonists, four times our number, wiped out overnight and just a few months after Squanto died Massasoit informs us that we are about to be attacked by the Massachusetts tribe. They are his biggest rivals but also a major trading partner that Squanto had made inroads with for us and who he had told me we needed to keep onside. Massasoit is either keen to strengthen his own position and get rid of any potential rivals or is simply holding to the letter of the peace treaty and demanding we protect him. The threat seemed authentic, though, as Standish said he had heard some of the Massachusetts tribe talking dismissively about the English and he thought like Massasoit—attack was always the best form of defence. But if we are to attack first, we are doing it on hearsay and not any real threats. It's lonely being the ultimate decision-maker and this is the moment I really missed having Squanto by my side. I know he would have thought of a political answer rather than a physical confrontation because he understood the tribes in question. He might have even found some point of negotiation. I don't know, but as he would say, '*What's gone and what's past help, should be past grief.*'[6] But I was and still am grieving for Squanto. I was desperate to talk to him but was then alone when it came to these difficult decisions. There was no one else I could trust yet to understand the nuances of tribal politics, so mistaken or not I decided that we needed to make an example of those who would threaten us. I allowed Standish to do his worst but can't help thinking what might have been.

"When Standish first arrived at Wesagusset, where all the troubles were brewing, his worst fears are confirmed by Hobbamock who translates what the local Indians are saying. He is approached by one of the tallest local Indians who makes the major blunder of mocking Standish. Standing at full warrior height, he looms over Myles and tells him.

"'You may be a great captain—yet you are but a little man. Though I be no Sachem, yet I am of great strength, and my size matches my courage.'

"You know how sensitive Standish was about his height, so that was the first big mistake by the Massachusetts and then the chief Wituwamat foolishly joins in. He shows Myles his knife with a sneer on his face.

"'See this knife, it has killed both French and English men and it has no fear in doing so again.'[7]

"Frankly, it probably took all of Myles' self-control not to lash out at this point, but as he has Hobbamock translating now, it's a much slower process than with Squanto so he cannot react immediately. However, he wants revenge, so that night together with Hobbamock, he works out a plan of attack. The next day he invites both men back into the settlement for a meal and makes a great show of not having any guns. The warriors are accompanied by two friends and some women. Alongside Standish; there are three other Pilgrims and Hobbamock who Wituwamat recognises with a nod as a fellow warrior pniese. Once the Indians had all sat down, Myles signals for the doors to be locked, and the battle begins. He grabs the Indians own knives and begins stabbing them furiously. Later he described to me how it was incredible just how many wounds those two warriors received before they buckled. He had never in his life had to stab men so many times before they stopped fighting back, all they had to defend themselves with, were their bare hands, and yet in all that time, they made not a noise before they collapsed. All Myles could hear was the screams of the women they had brought with them. That day every other Indian in the settlement was killed, and Standish hacked off Wituwamat's head himself to bring back as a deterrent to others. This is the first time we have Indian blood on our hands. The leader of the alleged plot—the enemy of Massasoit and Hobbamok, has been killed. The settlement of Wessagusset, which Standish had, in theory, been trying to protect, is all but abandoned and the attack causes widespread panic among all the other Native Americans tribes throughout the region. Villages are deserted and, for some time, we have great difficulty reviving any trade at all."

William is racked with painful heaving coughs now and John passes him some water.

"When he heard about the incident back in Leiden our old pastor John Robinson sent me a letter and every word of reproach is still burned on my mind: '*Oh, how happy a thing had it been if you had converted some before you had killed any! Besides, were blood is once begun to be shed it is seldom staunched a long time after.'* He was so right the poison never really went away, and that sense of unease and distrust at our very different ways of life exploded in the Pequot Wars when we pitted tribe against tribe just to keep trading routes open."

"But I was here then … Father, I was nearly 20, I heard all about those battles."

"You may have heard at the time what a great 'victory' it was over savage tribes, but without being there, you couldn't really know just how awful it was and how our own violence led to a poison that never healed. The Mystic massacre was a truly horrible sight one that I trust you will never see in your lifetime. At the time I saw it as the work of the Lord, as righteous vengeance but now I look back and wonder if we went too far. We were told that two English men had been tortured by the Pequot tribe but it just so happened that it was that tribe who were then trading with the Dutch, not the English, and the Puritans in Massachusetts Bay were very keen to acquire more favourable trading conditions and access to Pequot land. I was not an eyewitness to the Pequot torture but what we were told was not good. It was said that they made two English men suffer for hours. First, they cut off their hands, then feet, then they peeled off their skin with shells cooked it and thrust it back down their throats and then finally still suffering but alive they were roasted to death.

"The Puritans came to us with this story and so naturally, we wanted to join in their fight, and at the time it seemed justified. And just as Massasoit had sided with us when we first arrived to protect his tribe against larger tribes he saw as threats, Uncas the Sachem of the Mohegans pledged his loyalty to the Boston Puritans as he wanted his old enemies, the Pequots removed. Amongst the Puritans were several soldiers who had fought in many battles during the Thirty Years' War in Europe, and it was those soldiers who decided the tactics that day."

William looks up to heaven as if asking for forgiveness or trying to stop the tears from falling from his glistening eyes as he continues with his story.

"I remember it was a warm May Day just like now with the smell of blossom in the air. We arrived at the Mystic camp just before dawn; their fort sat on top of the hill and was completely encircled with a palisade—difficult to attack. We tried to enter but within a few minutes we suffered two dead, and half the soldiers that managed to get in were wounded. It was Captain Mason who then said: 'We must burn them.' He simply picked up a firebrand and set the camp alight and the wind that day did the work for us. We retreated and encircled the fort to prevent anyone from escaping, and The Mohegan and Narragansett formed an outer ring preventing further escape of any Pequot who might slip through the English line. Mason's men then lined up to shoot or hack anyone who attempted to escape the inferno, and in just one hour, more than 400 Pequot men, women, and children were killed. I will never forget the screams. It was a fearful sight to see them frying in the fire, or dying by sword as they tried to escape and the stream of blood mixed into the flames was the most horrible stench, it was just too much for me and I never want a son of mine to witness the horrors I saw. I told myself then it was God's work but it was only the English who were killing. The Narragansetts who had come to support us in a fair battle, stood back horrified at what they saw. Why did we need to kill the women and children? They told us to stop. '*Mach it, mach it,*' but the slaughter continued …so many innocent souls lying gasping on the ground."[8]

William's cough racks him again or is it more of a strangled sob, John can see his weakened father heaving into a rag and his face is red and damp when it emerges.

"Chief Miantonomoh of the Narragansett was the young brave who had brought that snakeskin to Plymouth at the end of our first year. It was a severe threat then, and he could easily have been one of our early enemies, but he had decided to fight with us on this day as the Pequot tribe were his traditional enemies. The only thing he had asked from the start though was that no women and children would be killed and when he saw flames destroy every living thing he angrily protested against the slaughter, '*It is too furious and slays too many.*'[9] He was right. Miantonomi spoke for all the local tribes. They saw war as warrior fighting warrior not total destruction. After witnessing this English savagery he wishes he'd sided with the Pequots when they had asked him to join with them.

"The problem was New England was turning into a race to grab land, by newcomers that made no attempt at being fair to the Indians who had always lived here. In just under twenty years there were now more Puritans in Massachusetts Bay than Native Americans in the whole of New England. Land and trade had taken over as the priority rather than living in peace. So many of these newcomers were not coming to create new communities for God as we had, but only for how much land they could take for themselves.

Our people were now just taking without sharing. When we first landed our vision had been to create the community of saints we dreamed of, and many of our Indian neighbours were happily coming round to our Christian ways. However, in just a few years so many of these newcomers made their priorities claiming land as a way to get rich without even trying to accommodate their new neighbours.

"Miantonomi has witnessed all these changes, and he now decides to plot against us and persuade other tribes to join him against the English. He travelled from tribe to tribe giving speeches about how his ancestors had plenty of deer and skins and coves full of fish and fowl. He blamed the English for destroying his land, cutting down the trees with axes, whilst English cows and horses ate the grass and hogs spoiled the clam banks, and he fears all the Indian tribes will be starved out of their own homes and he has a right to be worried about how little land was left for his tribe. He felt like many Indians that you could no more sell land than you could sell air it should be there for all to share.[10] However, he is captured by the Indian Uncas before he can start a war. Uncas had sided with the Puritans, and so he brought Miantonomi to our courts and to my eternal regret we washed our hands of the case and let Uncas do what he wanted. I am guilty of being a Pontius Pilate. Miantonomi was a friendly chief, he had kept the peace with us for twenty years, he had fought on our side and only moved against us when he saw his own homelands disappear and then witnessed what happened at Mystic. I allowed him to die with a hatchet in the back of his head. He was assassinated because of tribal rivalry when we should have been more generous and found a way to work with him.

"There is still deep unease and unrest among our people. Some Indians like our dear Hobbamock came to see the light before he passed over and others too, but many like Massasoit refuse to see our God and many new settlers have little of God's ways about their behaviour.

"John, I need you to promise you will help keep the peace because like Squanto you know and understand our people and the Indians. '*Qua patres difficillime adepti sunt nolite turpiter relinquere.*'"[11]

"Father, you know I don't know Latin."

"What our forefathers with so much difficulty secured, do not basely relinquish."

"You still can't forgive me or say the word, Father, can you?"

"When you first arrived I know you must have felt that I never had time for you but being Governor left little time for anything else, and your new mother was kept busy with a house full, so I was happy that you found companions."

"I was still a child, missing my real mother, you were always busy and I needed someone to talk to. Alice had all her own children to care for, the house was always full, and I just needed my own space. Every time I stepped outside the palisade, I felt I could breathe, and when you find a place you are always welcomed and listened to, it makes you feel special it becomes your home. So that's why I still call Hobbamock and Oiguina my American parents, it felt like I was back home with Granny and Grandad in Holland and that's why my Indian family will always feel closer."

"Hobbamock was a good man and became a good Christian and his wife Oiguina was also very wise. After Squanto died, I needed Hobbamock to be a better translator for us. No one could replace Squanto's fluency but we needed more help, and so that is why I was always happy for you to be in his house. Whilst you were learning how to hunt, he was learning better English and that is why I am telling you this story because on his deathbed Squanto asked me to take care of Oiguina."

"I don't understand."

"Oiguina was his sister and so although you never met him, he was uncle to all your Indian brothers and sisters and which is why you were the only child in Plymouth who was allowed to play freely with an Indian family. I thought that having you there would help them learn our language and Christian ways and I would always know what was going on."

"So basically you thought I'd be your spy?"

"That's not what it was about, I wanted you to be happy and needed to keep Plymouth safe and knowing Hobbamock and Oiguina were caring for you meant we always had an understanding between us."

"But there were strict limits to your understanding and as I got older you wanted me to distance myself from the family who made me feel loved. Even though Hobbamock became Christian, you didn't see his children as good enough companions for me."

"We are Pilgrims, John, and it was important that you married someone who was born into the faith."

"So being Christian was not enough, you had to be English?"

"You know my thoughts won't change on that one."

"But here is the reason why you are here. Squanto gave me this portrait and told me to keep it in the family. I missed him so badly when he died I couldn't bear to be parted from it and always felt he was part of our family, but he actually meant for me to give it to his own blood and with Oiguina now gone you must give this to her eldest Weetamoo."

"You've finally said her name."

"She's Squanto's niece and deserves to have her Uncle's treasure."

"Just as she deserves to live with the man who loves her."

"John, please just listen now, let's not go over old ground, you know what my beliefs are. If it is of any consolation, I think that maybe part of the reason I was so angry that you choose to love Weetamoo, is that out of all Oiguina's children every time I looked at Weetamoo, I saw Squanto's eyes staring back at me. Every time I saw her face, I was reminded of what I had so cruelly lost, and I couldn't bear the pain. You know that as a Governor, I have to make sure everyone abides by the rules but it wasn't just that you needed to marry an English girl, being near Weetamoo was too painful for me. So I ask your forgiveness but this is the story Squanto wanted his family to know, and you must tell Weetamoo how her Uncle's portrait came to be in my possession."

Chapter Six

Unlucky Deeds — Like the Base Indian, Threw a Pearl Away, Richer than All His Tribe

"Taylor, you look shocked."

"Grandma, I don't quite know what you are telling us now. I'm confused, you are saying William's son John ended up living with Hobbamock's family. That's Hobbamock who wanted Squanto to die because he thought he was a traitor? Hobbamock's wife who is an Ougina—like you—was Squanto's sister, which Hobbamock didn't know, and her children inherited this picture?"

"This is the story as it has been handed down from Gigi to Gigi. Squanto's sister was never given this picture, she died before William Bradford, so it was given to John who then gave it directly to a Weetamoo—like you—who was her eldest daughter. Weetamoo was the girl that John chose to love, but of course, even though Hobbamock had become a Christian and was living alongside the Pilgrims as the Plymouth Governor, William could not approve of an Indian girl as a wife for his son even if she was now a believer. [1] This was just not a relationship that William Bradford could ever countenance, as soon as he realised how close the couple were, he banned John from going to Hobbamock's house and spent a long time looking for a suitable English Christian bride for his eldest. What William didn't know, though, was that Weetamoo was already pregnant with John's child, which her mother hid and pretended was her own. And when John finally married to ensure his father's respectability was not compromised, he was by then thirty-three.[2] He and Martha Bourne moved away to Connecticut and the couple never had any children. Weetamoo, though, chose to live close by John with their daughter and it was to Weetamoo that John carefully told his father's story so that it could be passed on down the family line."

"So our family gene pool mixes the blood of sworn enemies?"

"Taylor, Hobbamock and Squanto were both brave warriors who disagreed and yes, you are related to both their families and William Bradford."

"But how can you prove all this?"

"All I can do is show you the picture and tell you the story that has been handed down as a secret from Grandmother to Granddaughter through the generations. Our family is the bloodline of that relationship between old England and Native America. Pocahontas wasn't the only woman to carry an Englishman's child. However, we who lived here have had to hold that secret close for four centuries because it was a disgrace to both our bloodlines that we are the result of two worlds colliding."

Sir Ian has been listening carefully, he places his hand on my shoulder in reassurance and clears his throat.

"You know, Taylor, you are in an exciting position now. You have chosen to study Art History, and have in your hand a painting that could be the proof you are looking for. If you can find the artist who drew this and date it to around the time we know Squanto was in Europe you will know that your great, great, great, great whatever Uncle Squanto, was the traveller he said he was. Then, if those dates link up with when Shakespeare was around to write an inscription on the back, you have a time capsule that would not only be incredibly valuable and link our two countries even closer together, but will be the evidence to prove your Grandma's story."

And of course, Sir Ian was right, it was a moment of clarity. I had chosen to study art and beautiful paintings like *The Birth of Venus*, created a century or more before the Pilgrims arrived in America. I was focused on what was happening before America even got going because Renaissance art and particularly Botticelli's work is about as far away from a Puritan sensibility as you can get. If old William Bradford ever gave himself time to gaze at such a painting he would probably have been less upset that Venus had got no clothes on, than the fact that she's not busy working at something useful.

Beautiful works of art have no place in the Puritan's world, so I didn't want to be interested in their difficult stories of nothing but struggle and hard work. Yet when you suddenly understand and feel that those people in the story are your family, it is a visceral, gut-wrenching moment and the subject springs to life through your own veins and bones. It is blood and flesh pulling you into the musty pages of the past, your own blood calling you to hear the story of where you came from. It is as if the souls of my ancestors are peering out through my eyes and skin to see where their stories ended up. Until today I had never heard that calling, but the dead are all around us in the bricks and mortar of our homes, the names of roads, staring out at us from old paintings and calling from the ancient standing stones that I had spent so long walking around with earplugs in. I'd spent my whole life ignoring the calls; probably because it was too loud a noise in Plymouth, too all-consuming, but now I can see that my choice of study was perhaps a way to find myself.

PLYMOUTH, MASSACHUSETTS, 1657 - BRADFORD'S DEATHBED

" ... Please don't leave yet, John."

"How can I know that all these things you are telling me now are the truth when you have kept so much hidden from me for so long and when you dismiss the rest of the family, so it is only you and I to hear your new stories?"

"Well, you don't just have to take my word for it, just a few months after the Wessagusset tragedy a new arrival visited us. It was Robert Gorges, the son of Sir Ferdinando, the Governor of Plymouth fort in Devon, who had given us the letter as we left, telling us about the location of our new Plymouth and what a perfect place it would be for a settlement. [3] Robert had brought with him a hundred and twenty settlers and a patent from the Council for New England which Sir Ferdinando ran, which gave him the magnificent title *'General Governor of the Country.'* He didn't stay long, though; he was Governor for just a year. They tried to settle just outside of Wessagusset and they renamed it Weymouth in tribute to the port they set off from. But, Robert was a gentleman who was used to being waited on John, so I don't think the hard work we live by was something he could ever get used to. However, he was keen to meet me on his arrival, and amongst the questions, he wanted to ask me about this new land, was where he might meet Squanto. In fact, I got the distinct impression that Squanto was the main reason for his journey. He was just ten when his father brought back a group of Indians to the family home. Gorges' plan was to teach them English, whilst they taught him about the New World. Gorges' fascination with these Indians turned into an all-consuming interest in promoting English settlements in America which his son Robert shared just as he had shared his tutoring with these Indians. However, neither he nor his father had actually taken the time to work closely with Squanto on the crucial lessons they really needed to survive America. If they had focused on the practical essentials of what to plant and grow in this new land then their Weymouth, and so many more settlements might have endured. Robert was distraught to learn that Squanto had passed away, and his sorrow when I had to explain the story of how we had lost him too soon, reminded me of my own terrible grief at Squanto's death. Clearly, he had been very fond of the man, having grown up with him and what Robert told me was that Squanto had always been inspiring. From the moment he'd arrived in Devon he'd shown great interest in learning about English culture. He didn't just want to learn the language though, he wanted to know exactly how things worked on the farm they lived on and how things grew. Not only did he attend school with Robert and his brother John but he often excelled in class outshining both and then would happily spend many hours showing them how to use an Indian bow and arrow and his way of hunting. Although he was most gentlemanly and courtly in his manners, he was also always talking to the servants and treated them as equals. He was eager to learn about animal husbandry and was most attentive and concerned about exactly how horses were cared for. I got the impression from Robert that he was much loved by all the family and he told me that his father and mother were not keen to let Squanto return to America whilst he and his brother were young as he was viewed as an extra tutor and essential member of the household.

"Robert also told me that his father would often take Squanto to London to excite interest with wealthy merchants and the royal court with the hope of them investing in these expensive New World undertakings, but he wrote me a note, which you must have:

It is with great sadness that I am informed about the death of Squanto who was a true and faithful friend of the Gorges family for many years. I confirm that the portrait in your possession is a good likeness of Squanto and that it was painted and given to my father on one of his many visits to London and that he gave it freely as a gift to Squanto with thanks for his excellent service when he departed for New England in 1614 with John Smith on what my father thought would be his final journey home.

"But sadly, it wasn't his final journey across the sea, John. After he had helped map the coastline with John Smith, he was kidnapped by the wicked Captain Thomas Hunt who was in charge of the second ship and sold as a slave in Spain.[4] Amazingly he was rescued by Friars who kept him safe in their monastery and from Malaga he was able to get safe passage back to London where he found work with John Slany of Cornhill in the city of London. John was secretary of the Newfoundland Company and a member of the Merchant Taylors' Company and decided that Squanto could be usefully employed as a translator in Newfoundland.[5] It was there that he was reunited with Captain Thomas Dermer who remembered him from the John Smith voyage and it was then at Dermer's request that Sir Ferdinando financed yet another expedition back to New England, to ensure his beloved Squanto could finally get home, just before we set sail in *The Mayflower*.[6]

"What I now understand is that Squanto's experiences were so totally unique: only he could have saved our people from certain death in a new and unfamiliar land. He had spent nearly fifteen years travelling and working with courtiers and city traders; he understood the world of business and politics at the highest level and knew how to negotiate with Europeans and his own people. Yet more importantly for us at first, he also had the most practical of skills most of us lacked, this was his land, and he knew how to survive here. When we arrived most of us had a trade which had been useful back in Leiden. There we had learned how to weave, print and even make watches, a few of us were carpenters but for our immediate survival what we needed was farming experience, and that was sadly lacking. It was Squanto who grew up here, who knew how difficult this sea-sodden soil is to work with. The crops we had brought with us all failed miserably and he carefully showed us how to sow Indian corn, without which, even those who had lasted through a winter of illness would have succumbed to starvation.[7] He told us how we could increase the crop yield by using hillsides, not just the flat river land. Instead of ploughing deep furrows, we were taught how to make small mounds of soil in which to place the seeds and then when the corn sprouted, to raise the soil to protect against birds. He then showed us how to add bean seeds to the same mounds so that their stalks supported the bean runners. Then we would train squash vines along the mounds to protect the corn stalk roots and reduce weeds. We would never have thought to combine three plants in the same piles; it all looked very messy to an English farmer's son, but this new way of farming was to be our lifesaver.[8] He also told us that in Devon he had seen how they put seaweed on the crops to help them grow and in Newfoundland, they add fish heads, and because he had grown up on this soil, he knew it was so poor, crops needed all the help they could get. The difference this made was the miracle we needed. He also had to show all of us how to fish and build weirs—can you imagine not one of us had thought to bring one bit of fishing equipment to a land of rivers, lakes and plentiful seafood? We thought clams, eels and lobsters were not edible: what a mistake that was when we were starving all winter before he arrived!

"But even more than our own day to day survival he saw the bigger picture. Having worked in the city, he knew we needed to trade to survive and pay back our loans, and he realised the biggest tribe had the most abundant supply of furs that we needed. Difficult to believe, but not one of us had seen a beaver skin before Squanto told us how valuable a market there was for fur. He knew we couldn't just rely on Massasoit for the future, he understood the business of merchants and that combination of native and English skills was what we needed to stay alive. What Massassoit saw as a betrayal by talking to a tribe that had always been his natural enemies, Squanto saw as a trade that he knew was essential for our survival. Squanto brought our two cultures together, but I didn't do enough to protect him from local rivalries, and it is a mistake I will always regret for the rest of what life I have left. I have missed his wise counsel so much. He looked after me like an older brother."

New Zealand,
June 2012

Dear Taylor,

All these extra facts you are unearthing in your research to back up Gigi's stories make it an even more riveting read. I am so looking forward to catching up in person when we can properly "talk story." I only have a few more days shooting to go here and then we'll be meeting up in Olde England where I trust we can visit all those places your ancestors stayed.

The tickets should be with you shortly. Remember to tell Gigi that she will be able to carry the painting and Gorges' letter with her in hand luggage. There will be no need to worry as she can keep them on her at all times. Just don't pack any drink, though, even if needed, as it will be confiscated. If Gigi is feeling nervous just reassure her, they do serve proper drinks on the flight.

Sutton Harbour,
Plymouth, Devon, July 2012

"On the top step, Taylor, both of you together and ... smile."

If you had told me two years ago that my Grandma was going to become best mates with one of the world's most famous actors I would have known I was dreaming. Yet the last twenty months have been full of nothing but surprising discoveries that constantly made me readjust my focus. Although Sir Ian has been busy filming on the other side of the world, despite the sixteen-hour time difference, he has kept in touch and was just as interested and fascinated by our discoveries as if it was his own family. I often think his love of Shakespeare is such a strong pull in his life that I wouldn't be surprised to discover that he is actually a distant relative of Shakespeare himself. Finding the truth about your family history does completely change your perception, and your discoveries make you feel that you will never be quite the same again but in a good way. Understanding just how many sacrifices your ancestors made in order for you to be here today, makes you appreciate what a miracle your own existence is.

So now having flown in from different sides of the globe, we find ourselves standing together in Sutton Harbour with a great sense of purpose. This is where my family story began: where Squanto would have walked up these stairs to discover a new land and where William probably reluctantly took the last step from his homeland to find his own new land. Sir Ian wants to mark the occasion by enthusiastically taking dozens of photographs on the Mayflower steps.

It doesn't take long before a crowd hearing his voice all want selfies but although Sir Ian is magnanimous when Gandalf says it's now time to move on such is his authority they all do so!

"So breathe it all in, you two, these are the historic steps that took the Pilgrims onto *The Mayflower* and the ones that Squanto walked up to discover a new world. Although since then Hitler did his best to smash up most of Plymouth at least this area around the Barbican is still amazingly intact with Elizabethan buildings, cobblestones and even a few old tall sailing ships in the harbour to add to the atmosphere."

"And what's that smell?"

"Well, Taylor, that's probably the most impressive thing of all, that is the warm aroma of freshly baked bread, and it's coming from the bakery[9] which stood here 400 years ago and gave *The Mayflower* its supplies." Inside the shop, Sir Ian hands out bread rolls like it was Holy Communion. A special moment as we share an experience familiar to both Squanto and William. "You can imagine the fear and excitement as William holds on to the last bread of Europe before what lay ahead and the sense of discovery for Squanto as he held something new and never tasted before in his hand."

Sadly all we can find of the Gorges estate that Squanto might have lived on is a ruin in a valley behind a housing estate. It doesn't look much now, but if you turn your back to the modern houses and look down to the river as it meanders into the estuary, you can imagine the view all those years ago. And perhaps you can picture Squanto thinking what a strange and different place it is that he is discovering, so many new sights and sounds and Sir Ian can't help to mutter Shakespeare as we walk across the ruins.

"Be not afeard. The isle is full of noises, sounds and sweet airs that give delight and hurt not." [10]

And his words spin me back in time.

St Budeaux near Plymouth, Devon, 1605, Squanto's view of the English countryside

Back home we think of ourselves as tribes belonging to the land, but here the way they use their land makes me question whether it is the land that defines the people or people who define the land. As a Wampanoag we see ourselves as people of the dawn, we are first to see the sunrise, and we follow Mother Nature's timetable. We carefully follow her moods, in winter we hunt, in the spring we fish and plant and in summer and autumn, we gather fruits, seeds, grains, and nuts. Here things are different. These are people who tame and constrain nature in ways we've never thought of. Here they want to separate nature from her natural ebb and flow and use their rules to ensure they have a constant supply of food and water whenever they want. At home there is a constant smell of salt in the air, and being so close to the sea there is that same smell here but it has a different texture, more earthy which I learn is the smell of seaweed mixed into the soil to ensure the plants they choose to grow are stronger than nature would provide.

Ferdinando was very keen to show me his cousin's work; they call it Drake's Leat, a man-made stream that flows all the way from the moors high above Plymouth along a stone-lined channel down through the valleys so that the city always has enough to drink. [11] Then there are the wind trees they have built, these rooms with wings, have branches which spin in the wind and inside a tree trunk which turns and cleverly grinds grain. I am impressed, at home we work around our mountains and rivers and trees, we grind our grain by hand, here, they dam the rivers, flatten the hills, use the wind to crush their wheat and move the trees to build their homes and grow their crops. Every day you can see yet more trees being removed to build the town's houses and I wonder how quickly trees grow here so they can be sure to replace the forest?

Ferdinando's tribal home is nestled in a valley just two hills away from town, the running stream and trees surrounding his building of stone, make the camp look as if it grew out of the rocks itself. But what makes the biggest impression on me are the fences and stone walls that clearly mark the land his family keep to themselves. Back home we have no boundaries: we all share the land. Or maybe the walls are only here just to keep the sheep away, the sheer numbers of these animals wandering everywhere, are staggering. It must easily be double the number of sheep to people.[12] They are amusing creatures, with shaky voices, they look like fluffy clouds with legs and yet I am told they provide everyone with all their clothes and meat. What I am thinking, though, is how come this land does not have wolves or bears like at home? One field of those little woolly beasts look such easy prey. I ask Ferdinando and he tells me that there were never many bears and you only see them chained up for entertaining the crowds now and that hunters got rid of the wolves many hundreds of years ago. Part of me feels sad these noble animals no longer have a home in this land.[13]

The rest of their tribe do not seem to be kinsfolk but work for the family—looking after their animals and cooking, and they have separate rooms and tables in which they eat.[13] Maybe the hunting is not as plentiful in this land, but back home we do not have to share our home with animals, they wonder wild and free, and we travel to where we find them and fish and stalk as we need. Here their cows and pigs and chickens rely on their human family to feed them. These are different ways, but I can see the attraction of knowing there are always fresh eggs and meat when needed, rather than wait until hunger calls. These people are so sure that the land will always provide they set down permanent roots. They build big solid homes around huge chimney fires and have different spaces for food preparing and eating. And it seems that each animal has its own servants, there are the dairymaids who milk the cows, the groomsmen who look after the noble horses, shearers who take the wool off the sheep and they even have a man whose job it is to catch rats. [14] [15] We live more lightly on the land, but these people have decided the land must provide their needs whatever the time of year and force it to their will.

And yet when it is harvest time just like at home, everyone joins in. They use big curved blades and work in groups around the field, working from the outside into the centre. I understand that it is essential that it is done this way so that by the time the middle of the field is reached the spirit of the crop has had time to move into the final sheaf and they shout out special words to say they have the spirit of the corn. They then chose someone who has to be blind-folded to throw the sickle at the sheaf until it is cut, then this corn is made into a human shape—a corn dolly, and it is kept inside the house to protect the family over winter, and the following spring it will be ploughed back into the soil to teach next year's crop how to grow.[16]

We may have different attitudes and ceremonies for the spirit of the land, but death is just as painful here as it is at home. And just like at home, the pain can only be soothed by observing the proper rituals. I have been enjoying learning with Ferdinando's young boys John and Robert; their little sisters Ellen and Honoria are too young for school yet, but Honoria, who has only just learned to walk, is very keen to be a friend.[17] She holds me by the hand when class is finished and takes me to see her favourite chickens and pet rab-bit. It isn't long before Honoria has explained to me without words that she understands she is not staying long in this world and that her mother and father will be sad when she leaves and that I must make sure her father can properly say goodbye.

One night when Ferdinando is travelling on business we are woken by crying and sobbing. Honoria has stopped breathing and is on her way out of this world. Ann, her mother is distraught and her maid upset. They send for their medicine man who says nothing can be done and then moves to take the body away. Both boys have awoken now, and Robert tells me that this man says his father owes him money and he will take the body of Honoria as hos-tage until his bills are paid. I know now why Honoria made me promise—I close the door, put a hand on the man's shoulder and shake my head. I can see he is a learned man, but there is no generosity of spirit in those eyes, however he is wise enough to know he can't match my strength and sullenly leaves the room. I stay on guard with Dehanada to ensure mother and child are safe through the night and next day until her father returns. Whilst we wait I place a feather from her favourite chicken in Honoria's hand, and ask the boys to give her a gift, Robert makes her a daisy chain, John picks her an apple, her sister Ellen a dolly and her mother gives her a precious ring. Once we have given her our gifts we then take it in turn to sing songs of sadness in honour of the little girl. When Ferdinando arrives he is heartbroken, he falls to his knees by Honoria's bed and is more than willing to shed a lock of his hair into her tiny hand to which he adds a button he plucks from his waistcoat.

"She could never reach any higher, but she would always pull on my button to get my attention, hold it forever now, little girl."

Then they call their spirit man who prays over the body until it is time to return her to mother earth in their place of worship.

Ferdinando wants me to attend Honoria's funeral for which I need to dress in English clothes. His servant takes me to a room of costumes, and I try on shirts and breeches. These are clothes I see that are very different to the ones his people wear, they have rough wool wrappings, but the family have clothes made of very fine materials, soft to the touch and very pleasant on the skin. I know it is a terrible weakness to get attached to things, but I can see how in this damp, cool climate these outer coverings can give comfort and make you feel confident. I wanted to honour Honoria's memory as her parents chose, so I went to their church of stone and listened to their spirit chief. We sang songs as the sun shone through the coloured windows before we all carried her in a special wooden box and made sure her spirit was safely given back home to the red Devon earth.

PLYMOUTH DEVON, JULY 2012

"I realise that pile of rocks in Budeaux was not very exciting but next on the agenda, Taylor, is a house that would have been the site of some very interesting meetings, and if Ferdinando was using Squanto to persuade investors, he might well have walked across these cobbled stones down St. Andrews Street.

"This place is called The Merchant's House, it's over 400 years old and its first recorded owner was an Elizabethan adventurer, sea captain and merchant called William Parker.[18] He was the Mayor of Plymouth for a while and helped Sir Francis Drake fight off the Spanish Armada. He had also travelled across the Atlantic to Jamaica and Mexico, so when Sir Ferdinando Gorges was trying to persuade people to invest in the Plymouth Company, William knew exactly what riches lay across the ocean and he was the first to step forward and invest. and I'm sure you can just imagine the scene, Taylor."

Sir Ian is right, all I have to do is close my eyes, and I am there alongside Squanto.

WILLIAM PARKER'S HOUSE, ST. ANDREWS STREET, PLYMOUTH, DEVON, NOVEMBER 21ST, 1605 — SQUANTO'S VIEW

At the time I wasn't quite aware of the meaning of the gathering I was invited to. It's only now looking back that I understand so much more of its significance. All I knew was the unspoken urgency of how important this was to Ferdinando. Despite the death of his daughter or perhaps because of, he wanted me to demonstrate what I knew about other visitors to my homeland and explain what I could to a group of chieftains who owned many ships.

The main chief whose home we were invited to was very imposing. I could tell from his face and confident manner here was a man who could cope with anything you threw at him. Captain Parker was clearly a much-travelled mighty warrior and had brought ample treasure home which was all on display. His house was the tallest building I had ever entered, with seven rooms on four different floors. You could see the trunks of many trees across each room, and including the furniture, it looked as if it had taken a whole forest to make this building. The working and cooking rooms were on the floor we entered then the entertaining Powwow room was above and sleeping and privacy on the top floors.

Once Mrs. Parker had welcomed us in, the greeting drinks were served by a man whose skin was the darkest colour I had ever seen. It was like he had been covered in charcoal ash. I tried greeting him in the Powhatan language, but it was not his. However, I could see in his eyes that he was extremely fond of the Captain.

"Squanto, meet Ignatius. I rescued him from a Portuguese slave ship and he's been my best mate ever since." [19]

And the look they gave each other at that point proved to me they were true life partners.

"He comes from Africa; here, let me show you on a map."

He pulls out a scroll of paper from a cupboard with markings on it which are meant to represent the land and water around us. Ignatius points to an area south of here, and then Ferdinando points out the land to the west which is where my home is supposed to be. It all feels odd, to point west for home when in your own mind you believe your land to be the farthest east your people have ever travelled. We call ourselves the people of the dawn but all this time these white people have been waking to an earlier sunrise than us.

As everyone had now arrived, Ferdinando stood up and began the Powwow.

"No one in this room has to be told what lies across the ocean this is a city that knows. Most of our seamen have travelled across the Atlantic, and many of you in this room owe your great good fortune to the trade made over there. Sir Francis Drake, your late good friend, William, was the first Englishman to sail around the world. He set off from here, and his crew were all local sailors. We know what opportunities are there for the taking across the ocean but what we need to do is make good our case at court. We have to persuade the King that this is not a fantasy project but one that could bring our country untold riches and to that end I have enrolled the help of Sir John Popham the Lord Chief Justice."[20]

Unlike our Powwows at home, those in the talking spot can be interrupted at any point.

"And there's your first problem, Ferdinando," interjected the Cornishman John Rashleigh, one of the wealthier men in the room.[21]

"He's not going to have the time now, all the King wants is to punish the Jesuits and chase any Catholic who might have been involved in their plot to blow up Parliament. He will have all his focus taken up sitting in judgement on those who wanted to get rid of the King."

"Exactly, Sir John is working on the very thing that concerns the King the most and if as the Judge of the Jesuit Treason, he can resolve the problem and get rid of all those who plotted against him then he will be in good stead to ask for a favour. Before all these dramatic events I was with Sir John in London, Squanto here was with me, and three of his tribe Assacumet, Manida and Sagamore Nahanada are now living in the Popham house. Sir John like me is so happy with what these Indians have told us about their land that it has made him even more enthusiastic to encourage the King to allow those who know and understand the sea to secure settlements in America. And John Rashleigh, I know you can be cynical about royal involvement but your father was clever enough to get the Privy Council to compensate your family for using your own ships to help fight the Armada, it is just that practical, clever approach we need to set up the Plymouth Company. Influence at court but practical know-how. John, you know how the Newfoundland trade has made you a very wealthy man: just think what riches are at stake if we can create settlements over there. Hundreds of our local sailors are travelling across the sea all the time, and your fellow Cornishmen in Fowey and Looe are leading the way."

"Ay, that they may be, but they are there to do a trade—fishing—which is what they know and understand. There are not many farmers here who want to leave their land, and you may have found a friendly native who is telling you what you want to hear, but how do we know they are all going to be like him? There are plenty of stories of cruelty and violence over there and even cannibals."

"Squanto here is no savage, he is a real gentleman, and I know. In fact, I had great difficulty persuading my wife to let him come here tonight: she sees him as her personal bodyguard as he has protected her from unwanted visitors and she knows he is truly loyal. What you don't know, though, is that he is also the most wonderful mimic and can make the noise of any animal on our farm. However, I have not brought him here tonight to entertain but inform and what I think you will find even more interesting are the conversations he has overheard of travellers who visited his land."

Ferdinando turns directly to me now.

"Squanto, can you repeat those conversations you have heard back home?"

I have memorized the list of voices he wants me to talk in.

"Bonjour, Monsieur."

"Ah, so he's met the bloody French—well, my captains tell me though they are hovering around Newfoundland most seem to be travelling further down to the St. Lawrence River, so the English hold most sway in the area still."

"Hola, muy Buenos?"

"Don't tell me the Spanish are now heading north? You'd think they'd be content with having carved up the south? And most of our sailors still can't forgive them for torturing our men so, despite the King looking for peace, Plymouth is not a place that forgets that easily."

"Yes, the Spanish do get everywhere but more worrying still is the next one."

"Dank u wel."

"Oh, so now the Dutch are sniffing around."

"But what will please you most of all, John—is the next language Squanto picked up."

"Da yw genev metya genes."

Everyone in the room laughs particularly John and his friend the young Trelawney squire.

"Squanto knows a lot more Cornish than any other language. He picked it up on the ship over here, and as our cook is Cornish, he is picking up more just from being here."

"But if I can interrupt, here, Sir Ferdinando?"

"Of course, Sir Richard."[22]

"As MP for Plymouth we've only just got the King to agree to re-confirm the charter for The Spanish Company, so we can control trade between Spain and Portugal now that peace has been declared. As much as my travelling has confirmed to me just how much more wealth and new land there is to explore, don't you think the setting up of a company that is going to annoy the Spanish within months of a peace treaty is exactly what the King is not looking for?"

"I'm intrigued, Sir Richard, when you more than anyone used your ship *The Dainty* to raid the Spanish main and annoy the King of Spain as much as you could."

I can't deny that, but now we are living in different times, we were at war then, and now we are not. As a politician and Vice-Admiral for Devon, my job now is to keep the peace."

"Well, this is about peacefully creating new settlements for those who may not feel as comfortable in this country as others. We can all see how over-crowded our cities are getting and many young men might not see a future for themselves here and will be keen to make their fortune across the sea. We can also clearly see in the light of recent events that there will be a lot of Catholics who will be more concerned than ever about their future and on the other side of the fence the strictest of Puritans are also unhappy with the King's faith. The Lord Chief Justice sees a lot of cases brought before him that have made him think that the freedom of expression many are looking for would be easier found abroad. And to be truthful the King himself would be happier if those citizens who are unhappy with his faith were to find a new home."

"Well, then the King should be investing his own money then to help rid himself of troublesome citizens rather than expecting the rest of us to cough up and solve his problems."

"This is not about solving his problems—that's just a sideshow—this is about creating even greater wealth and trade for the West Country. You know what your ships are already bringing back here, and with a proper foothold across the sea so much more could be achieved. Yes, it may take more time than a fishing trip, but the long-term results will be so much more beneficial."

Captain Parker now stands up—his height dwarfing everyone else in the room.

"Well, you can count me in, Ferdinando, I've seen with my own eyes the treasures that are possible and your friend Squanto looks a decent chap. Sometimes you have to take a leap of faith—that's what Sir Francis always used to say and frankly without that spirit he would never have managed to sail around the world. You can tell the King the old Mayor of Plymouth believes in this and knows it will only be a boon to our city."

I was right about William, he was eager to support Ferdinando's plans, but the others were much more circumspect, particularly John Rashleigh, he felt it was the big Chief's responsibility to pay for such a venture and maybe he was right?

"Well, I agree, it's the future, but I want to see the King spend his money first before I chip in. He fritters enough away on those plays and fancy costumes he likes—just half his wardrobe could kit out ten of our ships!"

"Well, Sir John Popham has a plan. He has been invited to the Court Masque on January 5th to celebrate the wedding of Essex's son with the Earl of Howard's daughter.[23] It's all politics as they are still children, but it will be the place to be seen, and Sir John thinks if his mysterious guest is a handsome man he will be noticed. With all the drama of the Catholic plot, there has been too much to distract the King, and he is not taking any private audiences. However, Sir John assures me that an attractive, intriguing-looking gentleman like Squanto, when dressed in courtier's clothes, will ensure the King asks questions."

"You have to be joking, you are going to take a heathen savage to court? Well, you are right about one thing—questions will be asked—the first being 'Are you mad?'"

"If Sir John is confident—then so am I. You've heard him speak French and we think in courtier costume Squanto could pass for a foreign Ambassador. Whilst everyone at court is obsessed with finding out who the Gunpowder plotters are, trying to propose a charter is not going to be on the agenda, so we are going to have to be bold and try something different to attract the King's attention. James may be imagining plots all around him but he will always notice an attractive young man. Squanto's English is passable—he is schooling with my sons, and in the right clothes, he will pass muster. Squanto, what do you say?"

I knew at this point that was my cue to repeat exactly what the last speaker had said—and so I produced my party trick.

"Well, you are right about one thing—questions will be asked—the first being 'Are you mad?'"

Again there was a lot of laughter and the Cornishman John Rashleigh looked at me askance.

"Gorges, you are playing tricks on us—do I really sound like that?"

John Trelawney had been laughing more than anyone.

"Afraid so, neighbour, you are a country bumpkin and you'll never pass muster at court!"

"I think I'd rather hear the animal noises!"

Chapter Seven

THAT IT SHOULD COME TO THIS?

Sir Ian stood back as Gigi and I took in the scene around us.

We just needed to stand quietly and feel the energy of a building that had been standing for over four hundred years. Quietly absorbing the atmosphere and imagining the scenes from when this house smelled of new wood and paint.

"And when you are ready, Taylor, I have one more piece of the Plymouth puzzle to show you, we need to head to the museum which has got a manuscript copy of the Royal Charter granted for the creation of the Plymouth Company and it's dated April 10th, 1606.[1] As the project was instigated by Sir Gorges, the members were all friends or relatives of Sir Gorges and Sir Popham, so the signatories included Captain William Parker whose house we are in and Sir John's nephew George Popham who went on to found the Popham colony.

"What's interesting about Sir Gorges, is that despite being the Governor of the Fort of Plymouth and having a critical military role, as a younger son of modest means Sir Gorges would always have been on the outskirts of high society. He had very little wealth and the property he had came from his wife, but he was a man with a plan and consistently enthused about America even though he never really had the funds himself and had to rely on wealthy and connected friends to supply the means for his plans and he had lots of plans for colonization. Which means in just a few months of Squanto arriving in

England, Sir Ferdinando had persuaded the Lord Chief Justice and friends to convince the King to create a Royal charter for exploring America all at a time when the royal court was consumed by the domestic politics of the Catholic plot to blow up Parliament."

LONDON, ENGLAND, 5TH JANUARY 1606 – SIR JOHN POPHAM'S HOUSE – SQUANTO'S VIEW

It was a very long night, and by the time we got back to Sir John's house, although I could tell Ferdinando had been sleeping, he was not going to let us go to bed until he had heard everything about the evening from Sir John.

"Well, I think we just about got away with it, although when we arrived, I thought the game was up as the very first person we bumped into was Henry Wriothesley. Now the Earl of Southampton is someone we definitely want on side, but I forgot, although he sponsored Captain Weymouth's exploration and has met the Indians in my house, he hadn't actually met Squanto.[2] So although he did look at us quizzically, as agreed, Squanto simply bowed and nodded politely, which did the trick and we took to our seats. The King was up on a raised dais right in the middle of the room, and then everyone in order of importance was sat on different level platforms down to the floor. In fact, watching the King, and his court, in all their finery, is as much of the spectacle as watching Ben Johnson's masque.[3] Indeed I have to admit I wasn't listening to the words as much as watching the extravagant staging and costumes. There was a huge rotating globe that descended to reveal eight men with swords then a beautiful lady dressed in blue and sparkling with stars emerges from the top and stops them from fighting and brings on peacocks and eight beautiful women who then dance around the men. The sets are simply amazing and really make you imagine you are in a different world; that Inigo Jones is a very talented man, but your Cornish friends are right: any one of those outfits could pay for a ship's crew, it has to have been the most sumptuous and intricate masque the court has ever seen. [4]

"I have to say the dancing by the ladies of the court was most agreeable, and Squanto did whisper to me that some of the moves looked like the dancing the women of his tribe make when celebrating the harvest and he really liked the way their jewellery glittered as they waved heron feathers seductively across themselves in the candlelight.

"But as suspected once an hour or so of the performance had passed the King's eyes started to wander, and in the lulls, I did see him look Squanto's way followed by discussions between him and his courtiers. So I expect questions to be asked."

"So you think you and Squanto might get an invitation soon?"

"Well, nothing much will happen in the next few weeks because I am judging the Jesuit conspirators in Westminster on the 27th. I know the King will be watching then, as he must and if everything goes to plan all the guilty parties will have been judged and sentenced by the end of the month.[5] Frankly, who knows what the King is thinking currently, you can tell he's not a happy man but his eyes definitely had a sparkle when they landed on Squanto. We just need to be patient.

"But you know it wasn't just the King who was looking our way, Southampton's writer friend was there, I can never remember his name, you know the one who writes for The King's Men? I suppose he has to keep up with what his rivals are doing. Mind if I were that busy, I'd want to take a break. The King had his company presenting ten different plays over the holidays which they had to fit in around all their standard fare down at The Globe."

"Do you mean Shakespeare?"

"Yes, that's the one, yes, William, never see him without a parchment in his hand, I always feel I have to be careful what I say in front of him as it might end up in his next play."

"I know he's a country squire from Stratford, so probably not a sailor but, do you think he would be interested in our plans?"

"Well, he's probably making a good living at the moment, but he's in not in the same league as the Earl, who can and does throw money away at whatever project takes his fancy. But when he's not at court you'll find him in Southwark either at a playhouse or in one of those inns they all frequent, you know The Tabard or The George. Might be worth a chat, although I'd think he's more likely to head you towards Southampton's friends who have large fortunes to squander."

"A useful lead is always useful. If William is entertaining the King on so many occasions, he will hear news that could be of interest and may well have some information that would be of as much help to our ends as finance."

"But if you don't mind now, Ferdinando, my bed is calling and look at how Squanto's eyes are dropping, he's had a lot to take in, and I'm sure he'll tell you more in the morning when he's rested, but for now, it's sleep."

THE NATIONAL PORTRAIT GALLERY, LONDON, ENGLAND, JULY 2012

We took the train from Plymouth to London along the beautiful coastal route where the sea is so close to the rails the salt spray hits the windows. Although it was quite a long journey, Sir Ian had plenty of stories from New Zealand to keep us amused. Watching him and Gigi together was like looking at a couple who had been friends all their lives. They just get each other's sense of humour and obsessions, always bursting out laughing at the same things.

"Tell me more about what got you started on all this research, Gigi."

"It was a dream."

"Really?"

"I had a dream for three nights in a row when I was younger. It was a circle of faces, clearly Indian and they were all singing words, I didn't understand any of them, but two stuck with me. I began to wonder if they were old Wampanoag words, and that dream led me to explore what was left of the language and, from that, with the help of the tribe and a number of translation documents left by Indian missionaries, I began the Wampanoag Dictionary Project, rediscovering our language which has helped us discover our past.[6] The truth is that the Pilgrims didn't come to America because of religious persecution, that was why they left England. They were happily settled in Holland, however, they missed their own language and culture and came to America to bring up their children in a 'New England.' So although some might say it was religion that drove them here it was a loss of language and culture, the very thing the Wampanoag are still trying to reclaim after 400 years. Language is not just words. It defines a culture, its tradition and what unites communities, it explains their story and creates what that community is. To be able to see the world as your ancestors did is all embodied in the language. So, it's really the revival of a culture and a way of life. There is a very funny 'lost in translation' story I think you'll like, about one early missionary who spent a day explaining

Christianity to a tribe who all listened very patiently then when he gets to the discussion of how they need to be 'born again' everyone in the crowd starts laughing. Idioms don't always work in translation and the native interpreter had just explained to the crowd that they should all come forth from their mother's vagina again! Can you imagine the scene?"

Sir Ian was doubled up in laughter at this story.

"Yes, I can see the look of surprise on all their faces! Yet when you describe these friendly relationships between missionaries and natives, you wonder, how did it come to such a violent end with the Pequot War?"

"It was not a religious war, it was a war between two cultures who had a completely different approach to the ownership of land and who could be the rule makers and people who make rules often don't make allowances for those with a different world view. You don't have to go too far back in time until I find that women in my family had their heads cut off and put on spikes to warn others about what might happen if you step out of line. So my family have had to hide the truth, of who they really are for a very long time. But then I don't have to explain what that means to you."

"No, having to hide who you really are is painful. It's the greatest regret of my life that I didn't tell my parents I was gay. My mother died when I was 12, and my father when I was 24, so I didn't talk to either of them about it but then I suppose if I had at the time I would have been admitting I'd committed a crime. Can you believe until I was 30 you could still be imprisoned for loving someone who just happened to be of the same sex?"

Gigi and Sir Ian look into each other's eyes with a deep understanding and hold hands, I might almost feel the gooseberry, but then he always finds a way to bring me back into the conversation.

"Now Taylor, what I'm really excited about is our next meeting at the National Portrait Gallery. It's a wonderful building to visit at any time, but the Chief Curator, Tarnya Cooper, has very kindly agreed to talk to us.[7] Her particular field happens to be Tudor and Jacobean portraits, so she is the expert on this particular era which will help you with your thesis and I'm sure it means she will have a lot to say about Squanto."

Sir Ian is right about the gallery, I will have to come back on my own to linger over so many beautiful works of art. The queues for *The Queen Art & Image* exhibition were something else but not surprising when you are guaranteed to see Beaton, Warhol, and Freud in one room. However, on this visit, we are lucky enough to be going behind the scenes to a research room where Tarnya works.

As always with the Brits, polite handshakes are the order of the day.

"Pleased to meet you, Taylor, and I understand from Sir Ian, that you are actually studying Art History yourself?"

"Yes, I am, so it's inspirational simply to be standing here."

"Pleased you think so but there is also another building you might want to put on your list, the British Museum has an exhibition on at the moment called *Shakespeare's London* and there is one item that I think you'll find very interesting. It's a diary kept by a German tourist in which he paints a Virginian Indian in a London park around 1615.[8] I can show you on screen, but you'll see a lot more if you go and visit yourself as they have paintings of the early settlement in Virginia before Plymouth even got going."[9]

"Well, they do look thought-provoking drawings, Tarnya, but from what I can see on your screen they don't seem to have anything stylistically in common with our painting."

"Mmmmm, so I can be sure then that it's not an early John White painting then, interesting ... I have heard only good things about Savannah College, so you must have some great teachers. Have you shown your painting to any of your tutors?"

"Well, I took a copy in—Gigi doesn't want to ever let it out of her sight, and the names Robert Peake and Isaac Oliver were mentioned."

"Fascinating that is in the right time frame, and both of those artists worked at the Stuart court. In fact, we are just preparing for our next exhibition which features both those artists work. This autumn we are showing a collection, all about Henry the eldest son of James I who died at just 18. It's called *The Lost Prince, The Life and Death of Henry Stuart* and both Oliver and Peake feature.[10] If you look on this screen here, this is the Oliver painting with the Prince looking very dashing in armour, and then this is an earlier Peake painting which shows him as a young teenager in formal clothes drawing a sword in front of a stag. Do you think either of these painters looks like the style of yours?"

"Well, they've both got certain elements that look familiar but I'm only a student, and you are the expert."

"So, Gigi, am I allowed a look now?"

Gigi gingerly hands over the painting enveloped in acres of bubble wrap. Tarnya carefully unwraps Squanto, and I'm delighted to see a raised eyebrow as she carefully holds the portrait and lays it on her work table under a magnifying glass.

"Now I understand you have had this carbon-dated to around 1612 but as you will have been told the results are always plus or minus 40 years which means you are left with an 80-year range of accuracy. Currently, science has no reliable and accurate means for the absolute dating of a painting. So, much of the work we do here to determine dates take more of a sideways approach. For example, if you brought me a painting that looked like a Rembrandt but it included the pigment Prussian blue—I would know it had to be a later artist because that's a compound that wasn't available during his lifetime. So there are certain things we can do to analyse the paint used but immediately from one look at this work there are certain stylistic things I see which to my mind give away its authorship. Take a look at the curtains, and carpets in the background those are the distinctive patterns of an oriental rug and the curtains are exquisite silk. The detail of these background elements is all about ensuring the viewer knows these are the surroundings of a very wealthy client. In fact, this is such a distinctive feature that I have to say I think I know the painter."

"Really?"

"Well, there is one particular artist whose work regularly features such extravagant curtains, and in fact, if I take you to Rooms Four and Five in the gallery, you'll be able to see his work for yourself."

So our incongruous party with Gandalf to the rear, troop through numerous rooms, with varied reactions from members of the public surprised to see a wizard in tow, until we find ourselves in Room Four and all of us gaze up at the walls.

"Now can you see why I wanted you to look at this painting yourself?"

"It's the same carpet, Tarnya—it's identical and the curtains! Who is this person?"

"Well, the artist is William Larkin, but this painting is of the lover of King James, George Villiers the 1st Duke of Buckingham.[11] Larkin also painted Frances, Countess of Somerset, who married Robert Carr, Earl of Somerset who also happened to be the King's favourite before Villiers. So Larkin was around people who were very close to the King, but as the son of an innkeeper, he was probably not deemed of high enough status to paint the royal family himself. What we do know about him is that his father ran a pub and happened to be a close neighbour of Robert Peake, who was the portrait painter to Henry, Prince of Wales, whose work I showed you earlier, so it may well have been Peake who introduced Larkin to painting and got him some early commissions. The other important facts we know about him is that he lived in Holborn, and Blackfriars and was only active as an artist from around 1606 to his death in 1619, which if we are correct in our assumptions immediately slims down your window of time."

Sir Ian now looked visibly excited.

"This is amazing news chaps because one of the few facts we do know about Shakespeare is that although he lived in numerous places around London, the title deeds to one of his properties actually survived in the archives, despite the great fire. I can state categorically that Shakespeare lived just across the river from The Globe in the Blackfriars gatehouse.[12] So, I reckon as we know he liked to frequent the odd pub, there is every possibility he might well have bumped into our new painter friend Mr. Larkin!"

LONDON, ENGLAND, JANUARY 7TH, 1606 - SIR JOHN POPHAM'S HOUSE – SQUANTO'S VIEW

Ferdinando kindly let me sleep in a little longer the next day, and then I tried to explain as best I could what I had witnessed. The music and dancing and costumes were all wondrous, I am still learning English words so only managed to convey a little of what happened but I think the reason I was so overtired was the wooden benches. Back home when we know we have a long Powwow we sit cross-legged, and the soft earth supports us. I just find these benches have no give and my back just aches. So it was a combination of sitting upright in a tight costume and remembering to bow and greet people in the correct manner that wore me out.

Today, though, Ferdinando is keen to get out and find more supporters for his plans and he thinks we will be in luck at one of the taverns in town. Despite the bitter frost we walk across London Bridge, and he tells me sometimes winters are so cold the great river freezes over but when we get down to The George this drinking room has a wonderful warm fire chimney, so it's a pleasure to sit on these benches.

It isn't long before Ferdinando has found someone to talk to. He leaves me with a drink while I quietly watch the many different faces in the room. So many new faces to think about and try and understand their story. At home, we only meet different tribes when we arrange a big meet, but these cities attract people from so many different places you never know who you are walking past or sitting next to. At home, we know everyone, here you know no one, and you can just hide in the background watching the world go by.

"Master Shakespeare, I know we have not met before but can I buy you a drink?"

"Thank you, good Sir, that's an offer I will always kindly accept."

"And to whom do I owe the pleasure of my beverage?"

"My name is Sir Ferdinando Gorges, and I am the Governor of Plymouth Fort, but you may know my good friend Sir John Popham?"

"Indeed, everyone knows who the Lord Chief Justice is, however I do remember you."

"Really?"

"Well, you helped save Sir John's life during the Essex Rebellion."

"Well, it's a little more complicated than that."

"Isn't that the story of our lives, always more complicated than we want. The Essex Rebellion was a very strange time, Sir Charles Percy asked me if we would stage *Richard II* at The Globe to help nudge things along but the company wasn't keen. The play was already five years old and Queen Elizabeth had always been suspicious of it so we didn't feel it appropriate.[13] However, Sir John still seems to be in rude health and at the Court Masque the other night he was sitting with a mystery companion who is so handsome all the court is gossiping about him."

"Well, Sir, I can tell you more about that mystery if we can take our ale to a quiet corner."

"Please do tell me more."

"Well, that mystery companion is, in fact, my friend and he is with me here tonight, hiding underneath that big hat over there but before I introduce you, I need to tell you a little more about him. He owes his presence here to your friend the Earl of Southampton. The Earl sponsored a voyage to America with Captain George Weymouth who brought back with him some native Indians. When he landed in Plymouth he presented them to me, I kept two and sent three to Sir Popham. I have been looking after these Indians for several months, and in everything they do they are true gentlemen, they naturally act like courtiers so going to the Masque the other night was not a difficult task for Squanto: he is just always so composed and has the most perfect posture."

"Let me understand what you are saying. The Lord Chief Justice was completely convinced that this Indian native would be able to hold his own at court when I doubt he'd ever think of taking his French cook! How on earth did he understand what was happening?"

"This native has been taking lessons with my own sons, and we have been having conversations, he is a brilliant mimic so though he doesn't understand every word his speech always sounds fluent."

"Well, Sir, you and Sir Popham are very brave to take a risk like that. Why would you do such a thing?"

"Because we want to use these natives to show the King how much opportunity there is in America and how the people over there could help us found new colonies. We want to get royal approval for a new company to settle America."

"Well, I do know there are many people interested in these voyages, I am not a seafarer myself, but I am intrigued to meet your Indian friend. Squanto, you said his name was?"

"Well, Sir, being such a clever wordsmith, I would love you to meet him, and perhaps you can judge how you think his conversation may stand at court?"

I had nearly drifted off to sleep again in the warmth of the fire when Sir Gorges brought over his new friend.

He greeted me with a *"God Save you, Sir,"* which I thought would be safe to repeat back. And Sir Ferdinando's new friend smiled broadly.

"Well, I didn't realise he'd speak with a Warwickshire accent?"

"He doesn't, kind Sir; he was just copying your inflexion. If in doubt he repeats back what you say with exactly the same tempo and tone. In fact, his Cornish is pitch-perfect. However, most of the time I think he speaks with more of a general West Country tone."

"How do you find our busy city life here, Squanto?"

"Mr. Shakespeare wants to know what you think of London."

"Very busy place—many noises but many delights and though many loud none seem to hurt."

"You know you're probably not mad, Ferdinando, that's almost passable for a foreign courtier. This could work, but what you need to provoke a little more Royal interest first, is a portrait."

"What do you mean?"

"Well, the King can never resist the charms of a handsome young man. I was thinking if you have a miniature made to be given as a gift, it will be a way to remind his majesty of Squanto's distinctive appearance and make him think of your friend as an ambassador rather than a wild native of some distant godforsaken territory."

"How are we going to procure a painting?"

"Look, I don't have the sort of money you need from an investor, but I have an innkeeper friend to whom I owe a favour or two, and his son is a talented young artist who needs a break. He's constantly asking to draw my portrait, but frankly I just don't have the time to sit still, the king is demanding new plays relentlessly and to be honest I should really be writing now. So if I introduce you, two people might gain from this. William Larkin is his name. He lives back over the river in Blackfriars, but he's been trained by Robert Peake who works for the young Prince, so he knows what he's doing and just needs his first commission. So that will be my contribution to your adventure. Send Squanto to his studio, it's not shabby, he's got it kitted out with Turkish rugs and silk curtains, and we will get you a meaningful gift to give the King."

TRAFALGAR SQUARE TO SOUTHWARK, LONDON, ENGLAND, JULY 2012

And so Sir Ian, Gigi and I left the National Portrait Gallery, our heads full of questions. We walk across Trafalgar Square, avoiding pigeons, and Sir Ian guides us to Waterloo Bridge. Sir Ian simply loves the River Thames; his home backs on to it and he delights in sharing the views from its many bridges. Gazing at the impressive sight I can see how telling it is to walk through a city where the old and new sit comfortably alongside each other and look equally at home, every century belongs here. There's the 20th century concrete bunker of the National Theatre lit by Victorian lampposts along the riverwalk and just a little further along the new old Globe is built in exactly the way Shakespeare would remember from four centuries ago.

New skyscrapers dominate the view and throb with the energy of a modern city but they happily sit alongside The Tower of London and St. Paul's Cathedral and the whole just resonates with the stories of the many who have come before. The past is not erased, and you can feel the atmosphere seeping out of Tudor wooden beams and Victorian stone as they jostle with the concrete and if only we knew the right way to listen they might playback exciting moments in time. Bombs or fires have inevitably wrecked many older streets but those buildings that do survive, thrive and are treasured.

Sir Ian's personal tour of the Globe is a tour de force. His deep love of the language which links and yet divides our two nations is a pleasure to listen to. William Bradford and his Yorkshire Pilgrims brought a different more sombre, serious language to America. The Bradford book is fascinating, but it's very much his official "story," told decades after the events, written with history and his faith foremost in mind, so it does not have a touch of the English fun and humour that radiate out of Sir Ian or Shakespearean characters like Falstaff or Bottom. Bradford's story is to be honest so earnest, with every word, weighed for significance that it's difficult to find any whiff of fun in those early days in Plymouth.

"And so, Taylor, in this pub all sorts of famous people gathered, in fact, this part of town is supposed to be the start of the Pilgrims' route to Canterbury in Chaucer's day, so it's been a significant meeting place for many centuries.[14] But if you look over towards the Globe and block out the skyscrapers of the city, you can see how close we are. It wouldn't take long to walk across, just a quick ten-minute stroll, and you could be in the bar after a tough night on the stage. So I am pretty sure that it would have been standard actor behaviour to pop over here for a drink or two after the final bow. And who knows if Sir Ferdinando Gorges might also have chosen this popular place for a quick ale?"

If it was Shakespeare, who wrote on the back of the painting if he did meet Squanto did it change his mind about the "savages" of America? As Sir Ian said, *The Tempest* depicts Caliban as a "savage" which is how most people saw native Indians at the time and yet he is given one of the most beautiful speeches in any play which talks about the wonder and uncertainty of the world. A world Caliban might not understand but is amazed by. Is that the impression Squanto made on William? Someone who travelled halfway around the globe and viewed his new and strange surroundings with a sense of wonder?

Chapter Eight

HEAT NOT A FURNACE FOR YOUR FOE
SO HOT THAT IT DO SINGE YOURSELF

SOUTHWARK, LONDON, THE GEORGE INN, DEC. 1611 – SQUANTO'S VIEW

"If they lay out ten to see a dead Indian then now I've got a live one I can charge as much as I like, good Sir, and so it'll be twenty on your own and forty if you both go in. No coins no-show."

"Ferdinando, don't worry about the price I'm paying."

"Are you sure, William?"

"I'm sure, I've been in already, and I know Squanto will be able to speak his language."

"Thank you, kind Sir."

The landlord pulled back the curtain to reveal a large cage possibly it had been used for bear-baiting but now in it stood a tall, distinguished native Indian who looked incredibly strong, brave and severe.

Epenow hardly looked up but as Ferdinando entered he uttered the words "Welcome, welcome" in possibly the most unwelcoming manner you could imagine.[1]

Then he spotted Squanto and immediately started talking to him in his own language.

"Is that you, Tisquantum? … We thought you dead … well, you certainly have gone native here … All this time I've been consoling myself whilst squat, fat strangers come waddling past to prod me that no Indian brave would be seen dead in those white men's clothes and well there you are—the dead Squanto. Why do you let them dress you like that?"

"I chose to, I was not forced to. In this country, it never feels as cold as at home, so you don't need furs, but it's never as warm and being such a damp climate these clothes do feel more comfortable."

"So now explain—how come you are free, and I am in a cage with my legs in chains?"

"Because you were captured by slave traders and I am living with a family who want me to be free."

"Well, get me into your family I cannot stay one more day longer in this cage. You know what they do here?"

"Tell me."

"They are vile—in the evenings, they send women in while their men watch and they insist that we lie together. Of course, it is difficult when they send them in naked, and some are easy to be with, but I don't like others watching, and only Maushop knows how many children I might be leaving behind me. It makes me feel sick inside they are so messed up … they are not human."

"Epenow, they are so human, but some just revel in their cruel side. I was lucky I met kind people."

"Prove it."

"Look, here is what we can do. My family is led by a man who spends all his days planning journeys back to our homeland. I will tell him you can take him to a place with much treasure and he will be keen to send you back on his next voyage. How much English do you know?"

"I've picked up a few curse words to be sure."

"I will teach you the words he will want to hear, like gold and treasure, but first let me talk to him about getting you out of here. It won't be quick as I have a feeling the man who brought you is going to strike a tough bargain—negotiations will take some time."

"Ferdinando, can you not see this is cruel?"

"Of course, Squanto, it is shameful, I will go and talk to the innkeeper but I warn you he doesn't look like an easy man to bargain with."

Sir Ferdinando emerges from the darkened room back into the bar and sees William and the innkeeper in deep discussion.

"Ferdinando, it's sorted."

"What do you mean?"

"We've agreed on a deal."

"How?"

"Let's step outside for a moment, and I'll explain."

"Look, I know this man, he drives a very hard bargain, but this is the deal. He has my share of the box office at the opening night of my next play at Blackfriars."[2]

"Really, William, are you sure? That is a huge sum that I'm afraid I know I can't afford to repay at this time."

"I don't expect you to."

"But how on earth can I thank you?"

"Look, Ferdinando, you've helped me."

"How?"

"From that first night we met you know I should have been at my desk writing, but you found me in the bar because I just could not find inspiration. I was drained after the winter season and was honestly thinking I didn't have another play in me. But your enthusiasm just stopped me in my tracks, jaded player that I was, I hadn't seen such excitement in years and then your Squanto, well, he just sparked off a hundred ideas in my head at once. I'd been stuck in a rut and had lost the muse but hearing him describe how he saw our world in a new and strange language to his own tongue just jogged my writing fingers again. And since then, every time you pop back to London your fervour for your plans and Squanto's sage perspective always give me a fund of solace and new ideas.[3] You have earned this and besides no free man deserves to be caged like an animal."

"You are too kind, Sir."

"No, if only you knew how your total commitment to a plan and your kindness to Squanto, who others like our innkeeper tonight just looked on as a savage has helped me focus. You can't know what value I put on that. And when you are finally ready to let Squanto go home—as I can see that brotherly love between you, then you give him this—I had two miniatures made of your painting, and I've written a note on the back of them because you both gave me hope, that I thought I'd lost."

Sir Ferdinando is speechless, but the tears in his eyes show his gratitude.

LONDON, SOUTHWARK, THE GEORGE INN - FRIDAY, 27 JULY 2012

"Okay, you two, time to drink up right now, I wasn't looking at my watch. You know back in January I told you I had been asked to perform at a major event, well I'm going to trust you with my secret now because it's only next month. I am going to play the part of Prospero at the opening of the Paralympics. After all our chats about "The Tempest" it feels so perfect but that's also why our plans have changed. I know I promised you a performance at The Globe tonight but if you will *'let your indulgence set me free,'* something else has come up, and I just feel it's a treat I have to share. And to be honest, I think what you will be seeing will be as awe-inspiring to you as Squanto's experience of walking into The Globe 400 years ago. So, if you come with me tonight, we will be sitting in a large oval with 80,000 people instead of a circle for 2000."

Our whistle-stop tour is about to be blown out of the sky by a phenomenal 21st century event, a showcase of everything that makes this country unique.

> *Be not afeard. The isle is full of noises,*
> *Sounds, and sweet airs that give delight and hurt not.*
> *Sometimes a thousand twangling instruments*
> *Will hum about mine ears, and sometime voices*
> *That, if I then had waked after long sleep,*
> *Will make me sleep again. And then, in dreaming,*
> *The clouds methought would open and show riches*
> *Ready to drop upon me, that when I waked*
> *I cried to dream again.*

Despite the date being 2012, it was Shakespeare's words calling to us yet again from *The Tempest*. Sir Ian looked across the Olympic stadium, from the spectacle in front us and turned to smile at us as Kenneth Branagh dressed as Isambard Kingdom Brunel declaimed Caliban's words to the crowd. Here we were part of a great global gathering of nations, and the words we are hearing are from the writer whose words are written on the back of our family portrait. From our first chance meeting in Savannah, I am now sitting with Sir Ian at the Olympic Stadium, London, watching one of the most spectacular events I will ever witness and still it is Shakespeare's words that link us together.[4]

Even though we had been watching a bewildering array of British icons from James Bond, The Queen, Mr. Bean, and a Beatle, the spine-tingling moment I will never forget is when Sir Ian and I heard and felt our transatlantic connection through the language our ancestors shared 400 years ago.

It is only in the morning after the most spectacular night before that I can calm myself enough to read the programme notes by the director Danny Boyle.

"Caliban's speech ... which is one of the most beautiful speeches in Shakespeare is about the wondrous beauty of the island and in this case, Caliban's deep, personal devotion and affection for it and that was something we all felt going into the show and wanted to reflect. Caliban's words do not seek to define or dissect the mystery he experiences, but admit his own inability to comprehend them."

Boyle then writes about how at some point in their histories, most nations experience a revolution that changes everything about them. He talks about the United Kingdom having a revolution that changed the whole of human existence, and he links together the Industrial Revolution and the digital revolution, both sparked by British men, in his account, as events which had the potential to change the world for everyone.

He ends the notes with this thought:

> *But we hope, too, that through all the noise and excitement you'll glimpse a single golden thread of purpose—the idea of Jerusalem— of the better world, the world of real freedom and real equality, a world that can be built through the prosperity of industry, through the caring nation that built the welfare state, through the joyous energy of popular culture, through the dream of universal communication. A belief that we can build Jerusalem. And that it will be for everyone.*

And then I realise that even though he used the words from Shakespeare's *Tempest*, he missed out on the one major revolution that actually inspired that play.

Before the Industrial Revolution and the digital revolution, the British helped to headline the Age of Discovery. British sailors crossed the Atlantic regularly—this was the Elizabethan space race—as Europe rushed to discover new land and continents that actually weren't lost in the first place. But this was the revolution that created America. Wind in sails, faith that God will keep you safe and belief in a New Jerusalem.

In London despite the Great Fire and Hitler's bombs, layers of history are preserved to reveal the past from which the modern city has emerged, there are Roman Walls, alongside Saxon churches and Tudor homes alongside Victorian mansions, thousands of years of history are mingled alongside a thrusting new city.

And yet in America everything that might have been present four hundred years ago we seem to have erased. Our oldest cities like Boston are happy to celebrate their history, but they only ever rewind the clock to 1620 as if nothing else existed before that date. Clearly, people were living here thousands of years ago, but unless it's in bricks and mortar, we have lost all sight of their presence.

In creating a sense of what America is thousands of years of history have been erased to construct the idea of a modern nation that started from scratch when the Puritans landed in Plymouth.

Their idea of Jerusalem, of building a better world was the burning obsession that drove William Bradford on through incredibly tough times. They were evangelical in their commitment to a better world of equality and freedom between men. But they left women and natives outside of that equation and once William died the idea of sharing the country with the natives who had always lived here, was flung aside.

PLYMOUTH, MASSACHUSETTS, NOVEMBER 22ND, THANKSGIVING 2012

Gigi stood at the head of the Thanksgiving table heaving with food and toasted our annual gathering with its extra special guest, with a prayer from Princess Red Wing one of our tribes great storytellers.

"May you be able to gain the peace
that surpasses all understanding
the gift from the Great Spirit
as my ancestors did.
And may you be able to call the
Great Spirit to bless your cornfields
of present-day achievements
as my ancestors did.
And may you be able in this age of creative noises
and modern machinery
find the time to be still
as my ancestors did [5]

"After all your generosity this year, Sir Ian, we are more than delighted that you are our honoured English guest at our family Thanksgiving. To be honest, we feel now that you are part of our family, having helped us find the English part of our family story that was missing. When we first met, I have to admit that I was only interested in learning about facts that I could use to prove the truth about my tribe as we have had to fight for so long to be heard and a stranger from England with stories about plays and dramas from long ago appeared to be a distraction from my real work. But I have learnt that often the stories that great writers tell us can have more truth in them than facts written on a page and time and again the history we have been told can be more of a fiction. There are so many things that we don't know, we don't know because history is written from a particular perspective and so it is often the stories that we pass between generations that carry our eternal truths. So as it is Thanksgiving, having read our Wampanoag blessing I'm now going to read a piece from William Bradford's diary in your honour:

"Our faithers were Englishmen which came over this great ocean,
and were ready to perish in this willdernes; but they cried unto ye
Lord, and he heard their voyce, and looked on their adversitie, &.
Let them therfore praise ye Lord, because he is good, & his mercies
endure forever...." [6]

"Gigi, I thank you for inviting this Englishman to join you, and I feel honoured. I also feel saddened that after all our travels together and our discoveries about the great friendship between William and Squanto that their story has not really been told properly. If you read Bradford's work, he makes it crystal clear that without Indian help they would never have survived those difficult early years, and it was only peace with the Indians that allowed his community to thrive but when he died that peace he had fought so hard to keep died with him. But as the good bard would say, *"Let us not burthen our remembrance with a heaviness that's gone."*[7]

"You are right, Ahanu, we are here to celebrate, laugh and have fun together, but all that happened in the past has shaped where we are today, and we must not forget the truth. Remembrance of the past is often bittersweet. Our tribe have fought hard to remember the truth of where we came from and the poetry of your favourite writer Shakespeare, has always told tales that tell of a deeper truth. So despite having told his truth to his eldest son, John, William Bradford could not stop the misunderstandings and John died just as the deadly King Philip's War got underway. So only one generation later Williams' second son, William Junior, stood as a General for the Puritans across the battlefield from Metacom, Massasoit's second son, who took over his father's mantle. It was a battle of cultures that was a battle to the death which ended with the systematic destruction of our Wampanoag way of life.

"All William's instincts were right, all the land grabbing he saw happening with the influx of European refugees, led to a war which many historians list as the deadliest war in the history of European settlement—nearly half of New England's towns were attacked, more than a thousand colonists died and three times as many Indians and of the few left many were enslaved and transported to Bermuda, and most others fled as refugees.

"But times have changed. In 1970, my Uncle Wamsutta, the tribal leader of the Wampanoag, was asked to write a speech for the 350th anniversary of *The Mayflower* arriving. [8] He did what was asked and wrote an honest statement, from the Indian perspective, which was then immediately banned from the official celebrations. I would feel honoured, Sir Ian, if you would read this for us today."

"But surely it would make more sense for you or Taylor to read this?"

"Well, it would if we were as good an orator as you! But you have helped us discover that there is an American Indian voice that your greatest writer listened to and in return, we would like your voice to read our story. Besides, the DNA of our ancestors are hopelessly intermingled, your English blood is as much a part of our story as our Wampanoag and we would like to hear our story spoken with the voice of Shakespeare."

"I am honoured."

Sir Ian stands and reads the words he has been given.

"This is a time of celebration for you—celebrating an anniversary of a beginning for the white man in America. A time of looking back, of reflection. It is with a heavy heart that I look back upon what happened to my People. Even before the Pilgrims landed, it was common practice for explorers to capture Indians, take them to Europe and sell them as slaves for two hundred and twenty shillings apiece. The Pilgrims had hardly explored the shores of Cape Cod for four days before they had robbed the graves of my ancestors and stolen their corn and beans. Mourt's Relation describes a searching party of sixteen men. Mourt goes on to say that this party took as much of the Indians' winter provisions as they were able to carry. Massasoit, the great Sachem of the Wampanoag, knew these facts, yet he and his People welcomed and befriended the settlers of the Plymouth Plantation. Perhaps he did this because his Tribe had been depleted by an epidemic. Or his knowledge of the harsh oncoming winter was the reason for his peaceful acceptance of these acts. This action by Massasoit was perhaps our biggest mistake. We, the Wampanoag, welcomed you, the white man, with open arms, little knowing that it was the beginning of the end; that before fifty years were to pass, the Wampanoag would no longer be a free people.

"What happened in those short fifty years? What has happened in the last three hundred years?

"History gives us facts, and there were atrocities; there were broken promises—and most of these centred around land ownership. Among ourselves, we understood that there were boundaries, but never before had we had to deal with fences and stone walls ...

"... History wants us to believe that the Indian was a savage, illiterate, uncivilized animal. A history that was written by an organized, disciplined people, to expose us as an unorganized and undisciplined entity.

"Two distinctly different cultures met. One thought they must control life; the other believed life was to be enjoyed because nature decreed it. Let us remember, the Indian is and was just as human as the white man. The Indian feels pain, gets hurt, and becomes defensive, has dreams, bears tragedy and failure, suffers from loneliness, needs to cry as well as laugh. He, too, is often misunderstood.

"The white man in the presence of the Indian is still mystified by his uncanny ability to make him feel uncomfortable. This may be the image the white man has created of the Indian; his 'savageness' has boomeranged and isn't a mystery; it is fear; fear of the Indian's temperament!

"High on a hill, overlooking the famed Plymouth Rock stands the statue of our great Sachem, Massasoit. Massasoit has stood there for many years in silence. We the descendants of this great Sachem have been a silent people. The necessity of making a living in this materialistic society of the white man caused us to be silent. Today, I and many of my people are choosing to face the truth. We ARE Indians!

"Although time has drained our culture, and our language is almost extinct, we the Wampanoags still walk the lands of Massachusetts. We may be fragmented, we may be confused. Many years have passed since we have been a people together. Our lands were invaded. We fought as hard to keep our land as you the whites did to take our land away from us. We were conquered; we became the American prisoners of war in many cases, and wards of the United States Government, until only recently ... What has happened cannot be changed, but today we must work towards a more humane America, a more Indian America, where men and nature once again are important; where the Indian values of honour, truth, and brotherhood prevail. You the white man are celebrating an anniversary. We the Wampanoags will help you celebrate in the concept of a beginning. It was the beginning of a new life for the Pilgrims. Now, 350 years later it is a beginning of a new determination for the original American: the American Indian ...."

Sir Ian pauses and then adds: "And so now it is nearly 400 years on, and finally, *'The hour's now come; The very minute bids thee ope thine ear.'*"[9]

And as I listen to Sir Ian add a line of Shakespeare to the end of my Great Uncle's speech, I am transported back to the first time we met.

But now standing behind him as he reads the words of my tribe I can see all my ancestors behind him: my Indian family and my English family. We were meant to live together, and Squanto and William tried, but the divisions proved too strong. And now it is my role to tell the story of America's ancestry, the people who came before and still stand for the land they knew and loved across thousands of years and that cannot be ruled out by the last four hundred.

"William Bradford's story is the one Americans have been listening to but now I need to find a way of blending the story of both my bloodlines. The fact that I am here is the result of one generation of Americans that found a way of living together peacefully—the refugees and the locals who muddled along for fifty years whilst William was still alive before the divisions just became too big.

"My very existence is the story, and I am now the storyteller, every fibre of my DNA is intertwined with both Indian and English blood. I am the moment that English refugees met Native Americans and a new world began. Within me live the duelling elements of what helped to shape the America we live in today. '*We are such stuff as dreams are made on*' [10] and this is my story because '*Those who tell the stories rule the world.*'" [11]

NOVEMBER 1622, PATUXET SACRED STONES - WILLIAM BRADFORD

William rows to shore, the sea is calm like a mill pool there is no wind and the water clearly reflects a full frost moon. As he jumps out of the boat his splashes ruin the reflection but William is not looking, he is just struggling to carry a semi-conscious Squanto on to the stones at the water's edge. As he lays him down he puts his ear to his chest to hear the faint heartbeat.

"Squanto, it's not your time to die, I need you, brother."

He turns his face to the sky and looks straight at the moon.

"Why, why, why, Lord? Why do I always have to pay the price, why do I always have to lose the ones I love—you took my father, my mother, my sister, my wife, not Squanto, you cannot take Squanto."

Squanto raises his hand.

"Squanto, you are still with us ...."

In a very faint and fading voice, he talks slowly but very clearly.

"Look beneath the third stone, and you will find it …."

In the twilight, William struggles to find anything but then his hand touches some material. Wrapped inside some fading English clothes in a small oval frame is a painting of a handsome man in a regal outfit but at a second look, you can see that the man is not English that proud bearing is defiantly Indian.

"William, I have been weak … my pride made me want to show you how I could do a better job than Massasoit…."

Squanto is clearly fading, and with each breath, his voice gets fainter but he has a message for William, and he will tell his story….

"I loved my time in England, the clothes and the food. I loved the family I lived with, but I began to forget my Indian roots…love of possessions is a weakness, and I am simply paying the price of not being true to my people…[12] this is the gift I want you to keep safe for now until you can find the right time to give it to my sister or her daughter[13] …It is me in English clothes, so it is me as a failed Indian.[14] I failed to persuade you to let my tribe back into our sacred place and I failed to get the others to trust that you English wanted to live in peace…But you must still follow your dream, William, of creating your new world…I know you are honest and good, and I thought I was part of your dream… but if I am, then please find the space for my people…The land does not belong to either your people or mine…we are all equal in the face of God and when our time on earth is done it is we who all belong to the land…Bury me here in my special place, make it your special place too, to remember my sacrifice for you, my brother, and then I will always be with you in spirit…."

THE LORD'S PRAYER IN WAMPANOAG

N∞shun kesukqut
Wunneetupantamunach k∞wesuonk
Peyaum∞utch kukkeitass∞tam∞onk.
Toh anantaman ne naj okheit, neane kesukqut.
Ásekesukokish petukqunnegash assaminnean yeu kesukok
Ahquontamaiinnean nummatcheseongash,
neane matchenehikqueagig nutahquontamanóunonog.
Ahque sagkompagininnean en qutchhuaonganit,
webe pohquohwussinnan wutch matchitut;
Newutche keitass∞tam∞onk, kutahtauun,
menuhkesuonk, sohsúmóonk michéme kah michéme
Amen

From John Eliot. *The Indian Primer; or, The Way of Training up of our Indian Youth in the good knowledge of God, in the knowledge of the Scriptures and in the ability to Reade* (Cambridge, Massachusetts 1669).

> *"Reclaiming our language is one means of repairing the broken circle of cultural loss and pain. To be able to understand and speak our language means to see the world as our families did for centuries. This is but one path which keeps us connected to our people, the earth, and the philosophies and truths given to us by the Creator."*

Jessie Little Doe Baird – Indigenous Language Preservationist, Macarthur Fellows Program.

THE WAMPANOAG TRIBE TODAY

On September 7th 2018, the American Government's Department of the Interior issued its first Carcieri decision in which it refused to reaffirm its own authority to confirm the status of the Mashpee Wampanoag Tribe's reservation. This decision opens the door for the Mashpee Wampanoag Tribe's reservation to be taken out of trust and disestablished and follows on the heels of the government's refusal to continue to defend the status of the Tribe's reservation in court.

The Department rejected the clear evidence of federal jurisdiction provided in multiple federal reports (some commissioned by Congress), Mashpee children attending federal Indian schools, federal representation of the Tribe, and other evidence accepted as sufficient in prior decisions.

HR312, The Mashpee Reservation Reaffirmation Act, is a bipartisan bill that reaffirms the status of Mashpees' reservation and has widespread support from Indian country.

Passage of HR312 will prevent Interior from disestablishing the Tribe's reservation.

The Mashpee Wampanoag Tribe's citizens are currently suffering a massive loss of resources and services due to the current actions of the American Government. Millions of dollars of funding are being lost or delayed for a clean water program, children's education and critical community service programs. This Government action is also a direct threat to their emergency services, housing and substance abuse programme. These are just a few of the ways the White House is impacting on the Wampanoag community today.

https://sign.moveon.org/petitions/stand-with-the-mashpee

Pocahontas to her English husband, John Rolfe

Had I not cradled you in my arms,
oh beloved, perfidious one,
you would have died.
And how many times did I pluck you
from certain death in the wilderness -
my world through which you stumbled
as though blind?
Had I not set you tasks
your masters far across the sea
would have abandoned you –
did abandon you, as many times they
left you to reap the harvest of their lies;
still you survived oh my fair husband
and brought them gold
wrung from a harvest I taught you
to plant: Tobacco. It
Is not without irony that by this crop
your descendents die, for other powers
than those you know take part in this.
And indeed I did rescue you
not once but a thousand thousand times
and in my arms you slept, a foolish child,
and beside me you played,
chattering nonsense about a God
you had not wit to name;
and wondered you at my silence -
simple foolish wanton maid you saw,
dusky daughter of heathen sires
who knew not the ways of grace -
no doubt, no doubt.
I spoke little, you said.
And you listened less.
But played with your gaudy dreams

and sent ponderous missives to the throne
stiving thereby to curry favour
with your king. I saw you well. I
understood the ploy and still protected you,
going so far as to die in your keeping –
a wasting, putrifying death, and you,
deceiver, my husband, father of my son,
survived, your spirit bearing crop
slowly from my teaching, taking
certain life from the wasting of my bones.

- Paula Gunn Allen

"HOPE"

"Hope" is the thing with feathers -
That perches in the soul -
And sings the tune without the words -
And never stops - at all -
And sweetest - in the Gale - is heard -
And sore must be the storm -
That could abash the little Bird
That kept so many warm -
I've heard it in the chillest land -
And on the strangest Sea -
Yet - never - in Extremity,
It asked a crumb - of me.

- Emily Dickinson

With Thanks

Thom Axon https://thomaxon.com/
Jessie Little Doe Baird – Wampanoag Tribal Council Liaison
Lee Basannavar
Liz Calder
Genevieve Christie
Dr Tarnya Cooper
Lord Julian Fellowes
Matt Giardino
George Ingham
Marshall Ingham
Mike Ingham
Julia Lemagnen
Mashpee Wampanoag Tribe https://mashpeewampanoagtribe-nsn.gov/
    standwithmashpee
Sir Ian McKellen
Nic Nicholas https://www.indexers.org.uk/find-an-indexer/directory/
    nicolanicholas/
Occidental University
Sussex University

BIBLIOGRAPHY

Appelbaum, Robert and Sweet, John Wood. Eds., *Envisioning an English Empire: Jamestown and the Making of the North Atlantic World* (University of Pennsylvania Press, 2005).

Bailey Moore, Jacob, *Lives of the Governors of New Plymouth and Massachusetts Bay* (Gates & Steadman, New York 1848).

Bittinger, Paul W., *The Pilgrim Story* (Memorial Press Group Plymouth, Mass. 1940).

Bonfanti, Leo., *Biographies and Legends of the New England Indians, Vol. 1.* (Old Saltbox, 1993).

Brooks, Lisa, *The Common Pot: The Recovery of Native Space in the Northeast* (University of Minnesota Press, 2008).

Bross, Kristina, and Wyss, Hilary E. Eds., *Early Native Literacies in New England: A Documentary and Critical Anthology* (Amherst, University of Massachusetts Press, 2008).

Bruchac, Joseph, Ed., *Songs From This Earth On Turtle's Back: Contemporary American Indian Poetry* (The Greenfield Review Press 1983).

Calloway, Colin G., *Dawnland Encounters: Indians and Europeans in Northern New England* (University Press of New England, 1991).

Ceci, Lynn, 'Squanto and the Pilgrims' Society Vol 27 Issue 4 (May 1990).

Clarke, Ted., *Scituate Chronicles* (The History Press Charleston, SC. 2014).

Cohen, Matt, *The Networked Wilderness: Communicating in Early New England* (Minneapolis, University of Minnesota Press, 2010).

Cooper, Tarnya, 'Making Art in Tudor Britain. New research on paintings in the National Portrait Gallery' *The British Art Journal* (Spring 2009).

Cronon, William, *Changes in the Land. Indians, Colonists, and the Ecology of New England* (Hill & Wang 1983).

Davies, Godfrey, *The Early Stuarts 1603-1660* (Oxford University Press 1963).

Debo, Angie, *History of the Indians of the United States* (University of Oklahoma Press 1970).

Deloria, Philip J. and Salisbury, Neil, Eds., *A Companion to American Indian History* (Wiley-Blackwell 2004).

Donohue, Betty Booth, *American Indian Texts Embedded in Works of Canonical American Literature* (University of California 1998).

Drake, Samuel Gardner, *History of the early discovery of America and landing of the Pilgrims* (Boston, Higgins and Bradley 1854).

Drake, Samuel Gardner, *The book of the Indians of North America* (Boston, Josiah Drake, 1833).

Dudok, G, 'Inigo Jones and the Masque' *Neophilologus* Vol 4 Issue 1 (Dec. 1919).

Eden, Jason & Naomi *Views of Older American Native Adults in Colonial New England* (Springer Science & Business Media LLC 2010).

Eliot, John, *The Indian Primer; or, The Way of Training up of our Indian Youth in the good knowledge of God, in the knowledge of the Scriptures and in the ability to Reade* (Cambridge, Massachusetts. 1669).

Falkus, Christopher, 'Life in the age of Exploration' *Readers Digest* (1994).

Firstbrook, Peter, *A Man Most Driven: Captain John Smith, Pocahontas, and the Invention of America* (Oneworld Publications 2014).

Forgeng, Jeffrey L., *Daily Life in Stuart England* (Greenwood Publishing Group 2007).

Fraser, Rebecca, *The Mayflower Generation* (Penguin 2017).

Franklin, R.W., Ed., *The Poems of Emily Dickinson* (Harvard University Press 1999).

Gardner-Thorpe, Christopher and Pearn, John, *Drake's Leat: Safe Water for a City* (Amphion Press 2010).

Gebler, Ernest, *The Plymouth Adventure, The Voyage of The Mayflower* (Cassell & Co Ltd. 1953).

Gilmore Simms, William, *The Life of Captain John Smith: The Founder of Virginia* (Sanborn, Carter, Bazin & Co. Boston 1846).

Gray, Todd, Ed., *Devon Household Accounts 1627-59: Part I* (Devon & Cornwall Record Society, Exeter 1996).

Gustafson, Sandra, *Eloquence Is Power: Oratory and Performance in Early America* (Chapel Hill, University of North Carolina Press 2000).

Harris, W Best, *Stories from Plymouth's History* (W.B. Harris 2001).

Hart, Jonathan, *Columbus, Shakespeare, and the Interpretation of the New World* (New York, Palgrave Macmillan 2003).

Hole, Christina, *British Folk Customs* (Hutchinson, 1976).

Holt, KD, *Sir Ferdinando Gorges : a quatercentenary tribute, 1565-1965* (Plymouth, The Corporation, 1965).

Hoxie, Frederick, E. '"Thinking like an Indian" Exploring American Indian Views of American History' *Reviews in American History* 29. 1-14 (2001).

Humins, John H., 'Squanto and Massasoit a struggle for Power' *The New England Quarterly* Vol 60 No 1 (Mar 1987).

Jewitt, Llewellynn Frederick William Luke, *A History of Plymouth Vol 1* (Plymouth 1873).

Jones, Capers, *The History and Future of Narragansett Bay* (Universal-Publishers, Boca Raton, Florida 2006).

Kaufmann, Miranda, *Black Tudors, The Untold Story* (OneWorld 2017).

Kupperman, Karen Ordahl, *The Jamestown Project* (Cambridge, Mass: Harvard University Press 2007).

Kurlansky, Mark, *Cod: A Biography of the Fish That Changed the World* (London, Vintage Books 1997).

Lacey, Robert, *Great Tales from English History. Chaucer to The Glorious Revolution 1387-1688* (Little, Brown and Company 2005).

Laslett, Peter, *The World We Have Lost, further explored* (University Press Cambridge 2000).

Lawson, Angelica Marie, *Resistance and Resilience in the work of Four Native American Authors* (University of Arizona 2006).

Leonard, A. Adolf, 'Squanto's Role in Pilgrim Diplomacy' *Ethnohistory* Vol 11 No 3 (Duke University Press 1964).

Lindley, David, *The Trials of Frances Howard: Fact and Fiction at the Court of King James* (Routledge 1993).

MacGregor, Neil, *Shakespeare's Restless World. An Unexpected History in Twenty Objects* (Penguin Books 2014).

Marshall, John, *A history of the colonies planted by the English on the continent of North America, from their settlement to the commencement of that war which terminated in their independence* (Philadelphia, A. Small 1824).

Metaxas, Eric, 'The Miracle of Squanto's Path to Plymouth' *Wall Street Journal* (25/11/2015).

Mignolo, Walter, *The Darker Side of the Renaissance: Literacy, Territoriality and Colonization* (University of Michigan Press, 1995).

Milton, Giles, *Big Chief Elizabeth. How England's Adventurers Gambled and Won the new World* (Hodder & Stoughton 2000).

Molloy, Anne Stearns Baker, *Five Kidnapped Indians: A True 17th Century Account of Five Early Americans* (Hastings House 1968).

Morpurgo, Horatio, *The Paradoxal Compass, Drake's Dilemma* (Notting Hill Editions 2017).

Morrison, Kenneth M., *The Embattled Northeast: The Elusive Ideal of Alliance in Abenaki-Euramerican Relations* (University of California Press 1984).

Mortimer, Ian, *The Time Traveller's Guide to Elizabethan England* (Random House 2012).

Peck, Linda Levy, *Patronage and Corruption in Early Stuart England* (Routledge 1993).

Philbrick, Nathaniel, *Mayflower, A Voyage to War* (Harper Press 2006).

Peters, Ramona Louise, 'Community Development Planning with a Native American Tribe in a Colonized Environment. Mashpee Wompanoag, A Modern Native American Tribe in Southern New England Seeking To Maintain Traditional Values and Cultural Integrity' (Californian School of Professional Psychology Fresno Campus 2003).

Porter, H.C., *Reflections on the Ethnohistory of Early Colonial North America* (Cambridge University Press 1982).

Preston, Richard Arthur, *Gorges of Plymouth Fort: A Life of Sir Fernando Gorges, Captain of Plymouth Fort, Governor of New England, and Lord of the Province of Maine* (University of Toronto Press 1953).

Round, Phillip H., *Histories of the Book in Indian Country, 1663– 1880* (Chapel Hill, University of North Carolina Press 2010).

Rowse, A.L., *The Expansion of Elizabethan England* (London, Macmillan 1955).

Rowse, A.L., *The Elizabethans and America* (McMillan & Co. Ltd 1959).

Sayre, Gordon M., *Les Sauvages Américains: Representations of Native Americans in French and English Colonial Literature* (Chapel Hill: University of North Carolina Press 1997).

Shuffleton, Frank, 'Indian Devils and Pilgrim Fathers, Squanto, Hobomok and the English conception of Indian religion' *The New England Quarterly Vol 49 No 1* (1976).

Simmons, Williams, *Spirit of the New England Tribes: Indian History and Folklore, 1620-1984* (Hanover, New Hampshire, University Press of New England 1986).

Smith, Cheryl Coleen, *Out of Her Place: Early Modern Exploration and Female Authorship* (Tufts University 2001).

Smith, Linda Tuhiwai, *Decolonizing Methodologies: Research and Indigenous Peoples* (Dunedin, University of Otago Press 1999).

Stephenson, Henry Thew, *Shakespeare's London* (New York, Henry Holt & Co. 1905).

Stewart-Smith, David, *The Pennacook Indians and the New England frontier, circa 1604-1733* (Union Institute and University Cincinnati, Ohio ProQuest Dissertations Publishing 1998).

Sweet, David G. and Nash, Gary B. Eds., *Struggle and Survival in Colonial America* (Berkeley, University of California Press 1981).

Turner III, Frederick ed., *The Portable North American Indian Reader* (New York, Penguin 1987).

Vaughan, Alden T., *Transatlantic Encounters: American Indians in Britain, 1500 -1776* (Cambridge University Press 2009).

Walthew Rice, Douglas, *The Life and Achievements of Sir John Popham, 1531-1607: Leading to the Establishment of the First English Colony in New England* (US, Fairleigh Dickinson University Press 2005).

Weaver, Jace, *The Red Atlantic: American Indigenes and the Making of the Modern World, 1000-1927* (UNC Press Books 2014).

Winder, Robert, *The Last Wolf: The Hidden Springs of Englishness. How the killing of the last wolf in England changed the course of history* (Little Brown 2017).

Chapter Notes

[ALL URL LINKS ACTIVE WHEN ACCESSED]

PROLOGUE

1. 'The Hobbit's Gandalf almost proved a green screen too far for Ian McKellen' Pulver, Andrew: (Guardian 20/11/2013)
2. 'Sir Ian McKellen: Filming The Hobbit made me think I should quit acting' Daly, Emma (Radio Times 14/11/2013)
3. Ahanu - Algonquin for "He laughs" www.snowwowl.com (2001) https://indiancountrymedianetwork.com/culture/arts-entertainment/native-humor-friday-funny-roadside-jokes/

CHAPTER ONE
PAST IS PROLOGUE

1. Savannah College of Art and Design hold a film festival every autumn ranked in the top 50 by MovieMaker. They have had many honoured guests including Liam Neeson and Sir Ian McKellen who both appeared in 2010. The speech by Thomas More was read to the audience at that appearance.
2. The Booke of Sir Thomas Moore c. 1601–04 Anthony Munday, Edmund Tillney, Henry Chettle, Thomas Heywood, William Shakespeare, Thomas Dekker, unknown copyist. The British Library, Harley MS 7368 https://www.bl.uk/collection-items/shakespeares-handwriting-in-the-book-of-sir-thomas-more
3. 'What would Shakespeare do about Europe's migrants? Shakespeare had little patience for xenophobes.' Steinglass, Matt (*The Economist* 23/10/2015)
4. BBC News Headline 16 December 2010 https://www.bbc.co.uk /news/uk-

england-london-11990646

5. Family nicknames - Weetamoo = Sweetheart – Gigi = Oiguina – old Indian family name

6. "What's gone and what's past help, should be past grief." *The Winter's Tale*

7. "14 sayings only people from New England understand." Robinson, Melia (*Business Insider* Dec. 27, 2015) http://uk.businessinsider.com /new-england-sayings-2015-12?r=US&IR=T/#now-thats-a-new-york-system-hot-wiener-9

8. Henry Thew Stephenson *Shakespeare's London* (New York Henry Holt & Co. 1905) http://babel.hathitrust.org/cgi/pt?id=hvd.hx3ax7;view= 1up;seq=375

9. The Yorkshire Historical Dictionary – Cramble means to hobble https://www.bbc.co.uk/news/uk-england-york-north-yorkshire-46892232

10. Gipping means to vomit, noggin means head and noggling headachey or annoying. https://www.pennine-gp-training.co.uk/res/yorkshire _slang_glossary.pdf

11. In 1597 a 50 ship cod fishing fleet with 200 canvas sails, returned to Plymouth from the Grand Banks. p. 59 *Cod: A Biography of the Fish that Changed the World* Kurlansky, Mark (Vintage Boos 1997)

CHAPTER TWO
LOVED NOT WISELY BUT TOO WELL

1. Maushap to the people of the first light he was a kind, benevolent god, a warrior against evil who possessed magical powers http://www. native-languages.org/mohegan-legends.htm

2. George Weymouth's account of 1605 voyage http://www.davistownmuseum.org/InfoRosiersRelation.html_

3. In 1618 a comet appeared in the skies over Europe, signalling, to The Pilgrims that the world was on the verge of the millennium—the thousand-year rule of the saints predicted in the book of Revelation.

4. "it was not with them, as with other men, whom small things could discourage, or small discontents cause to wish themselves at home again" *A History of the Colonies planted by the English on the Continent of North America* p. 79 Marshall, John (Philadelphia, A. Small, 1824)

5. Governor William Bradford's description of Squanto in *Of Plymouth Plantation*

6. https://en.wikipedia.org/wiki/Ferdinando_Gorges

7. https://en.wikipedia.org/wiki/Thomas_Dermer

8. Thomas Morton who came into a lot of conflict with Plymouth and the Pilgrims on several occasions and was driven out of New England by them, gave this description of the area "and the bones and skulls upon several places of their habitations made such a spectacle after my coming into these parts, that, as I travelled in the Forest near the Massachusetts, it seemed to me a new found Golgotha."

9. During the brief time, Squanto looked after the Pilgrims a letter sent back to England described the local Indians in glowing terms. In one of the final sections of Mourt's Relation Edward Winslow writes that the Indians are "very trusty, quick of apprehension, ripe witted, 'just' and 'very faithful' in their covenant of peace with us. Very loving and ready to pleasure us. We often go to them, and they come to us …and we …walk as peacefully and safely in the woods as in the highways of England. We entertain them familiarly in our houses and they as friendly bestowing their venison on us."

10. Aiden T. Vaughan. *Transatlantic Encounters: American Indians in Britain, 1500-1776* (Cambridge University Press 2009)

11. Bruce, P Lenman. *Virginia's Father King James I* (Colonial Williamsburg Journal Autumn 2001) https://www.history.org/Foundation/journal/Autumn01/jamesI.cfm

12. James I. *Essayes in Poesie* (1585) *A Counterblaste to Tobacco* (Arber, Renascence Editions 1604)

13. "Grandma's Experiences Leave a Mark on Your Genes" Hurley, Dan: *Discover Magazine; Science for the Curious* (June 25 2013) http://discovermagazine.com/2013/may/13-grandmas-experiences-leave-epigenetic-mark-on-your-genes

CHAPTER THREE
YOU TAUGHT ME LANGUAGE, AND MY PROFIT ON'T, IS, I KNOW HOW TO CURSE

1. Albert Christopher Addison *The Romantic Story of the Mayflower Pilgrims* (1911). The Plymouth Colony Archive Project http://www.histarch.illinois.edu/plymouth/addisontxt.html

2. Christopher Falkus *Life in the Age of Exploration* (RDA Ltd 1994)

3. Uttamatomakkin, known as Tomocomo for short, was a Powhatan native shaman who accompanied Pocahontas on her visit to London

in 1616. Arriving at Plymouth, Tomocomo picked up a stick on which to mark notches to keep a tally, but soon grew "weary." *"This Saluage, one of Powhatans Councell, being amongst them held an understanding fellow; the King purposely sent him, as they say, to number the people here, and informe him well what wee were and our state. Arriuing at Plimoth, according to his directions, he got a long sticke, whereon by notches hee did thinke to haue kept the number of all the men hee could see, but he was quickly wearie of that taske: . The Generall Historie of Virginia, New-England, and the Summer Isles 1584 -1624* p. 123 Smith, John (Electronic edition University of North Carolina at Chapel Hill, 2006)

4. 'The 16th Century protection of Sutton Harbour & Plymouth Sound: Documentary Evidence. This article describes the defence preparations in Devon against the arrival of the Spanish Armada: So doth the state of this countrye reste quiet in orderlye readynes' (Brayshay, Mark. Prof. (Plymouth University 1996) in Gray, T. (ed.) Devon Documents in honour of Mrs Margery Rowe, Devon & Cornwall Notes & Queries Special Issue, 20-25.

5. Ian Mortimer *The Time Traveller's Guide to Elizabethan England* (Random House 2012)

6. 'The Real Story Behind Plymouth Rock ; Explore the real history of the Pilgrims' purported landing place—Plymouth Rock' Klein, Christopher (history.com Nov. 21, 2012)

7. "Action is eloquence" *Coriolanus* Act 3 Sc 2 William Shakespeare

8. Edward Winslow describes Massasoit sweating and shaking in *Mourt's Relation: A Journal of the Beginning and Proceedings of the English Plantation Settled at Plimoth in New England* University Microfilm (Ann Arbor, Michigan) facsimile edition of the original 1622 edition.

9. 'Good newes from New-England : or, A true relation of things very remarkable at the plantation of Plimoth in New-England ... Together with a relation of such religious and civill lawes and customes, as are in practise amongst the Indians ... by Winslow, Edward, 1595-1655' (John Adams Library, Boston Public Library)

10. Leo Bonfanti *Biographies and Legends of the New England Indians* (Old Saltbox 1993)

11. "I am a feather for each wind that blows" *The Winter's Tale* Act 2 Sc 3 William Shakespeare

12. *A feather in your cap: inside the symbolic universe of Renaissance Europe.* Rublack, Ulinka Professor University of Cambridge 02 Nov. 2017 https://www.cam.ac.uk/research/features/a-feather-in-your-cap-inside-the-symbolic-universe-of-renaissance-europe, Samuel Gardner Drake *History of the Early Discovery of America and Landing of the Pilgrims* p. 353 (Higgins and Bradley 1854)

13. Mark Kurlansky *Cod: A Biography of the Fish that Changed the World* p. 59 (Vintage 1997)

14. Richard Arthur Preston *Gorges of Plymouth Fort* (University of Toronto Press 1953)

15. Alexander Young *Chronicles of the Pilgrim Fathers of the Colony of Plymouth: From 1602-1625* p. 55 (Charles C Boston, Little & James Brown 1841)

16. Richard Arthur Preston. *Gorges of Plymouth Fort* (University of Toronto Press 1953)

17. "more gentle-kind than of our human generation" *The Tempest* Act 3 Sc 3 William Shakespeare

18. George Parker Winship *Sailors Narratives Of Voyages Along The New England Coast, 1524-1624* (Ed. Houghton, pp. 220-221 (Mifflin & company 1905 Collection of the Massachusetts Historical Society)

19. Execution by beheading is the just punishment for a traitor at this time

20. Aug. 14th 1621 is the date they go to Corbitant's camp

21. "Or have we some strange Indian" *Henry VIII* Act 5 Sc 3 William Shakespeare

22. "Damn you for teaching me your language!" *The Tempest* Act 1 Sc 2 William Shakespeare

CHAPTER FOUR
MORE SINNED AGAINST THAN SINNING

1. An abundance of seafood was rejected by the Puritans *Cod: A Biography of the Fish that Changed the World* Kurlansky, Mark. p. 69 (Vintage

1997) Even though they washed up on the seashore in two foot piles the English saw them as trash food. In 1622, the governor of Plymouth Plantation, William Bradford, was embarrassed to admit to newly arrived colonists that the only food they *could presente their friends with was a lobster ... without bread or anyhting else but a cupp of fair water.* And there are stories that a little later, some in Massachusetts revolted and the colony was forced to sign contracts promising that indentured servants wouldn't be fed lobster more than three times a week. Luzer, Daniel: *Pacific Standard*, June 14, 2017 https://psmag.com/economics/how-lobster-got-fancy-59440

2. Robert Lacey *Great Tales from English History. Chaucer to The Glorious Revolution 1387-1688* (Little, Brown and Company 2005)

3. The origins of Paul Simon's American Tune—the melody is attributed to the chorale from Johann Sebastian Bach's "St. Matthew Passion," itself a reworking of an earlier secular song, "Mein Gmüth ist mir verwirret," composed by Hans Hassler 1564-1612, a song popular across Europe before the Pilgrims set sail. www.songfacts.com

4. "..such sweet thunder" *A Midsummer Night's Dream* Act 4, Scene 1

5. "When the battle's lost and won" *Macbeth*: Act 1, Scene 1

6. James A. Warren *God, War and Providence. The Epic Struggle of Roger Williams and the Narragansett Indians against the Puritans of New England* p. 23. (Scribner, Simon & Schuster 2018)

7. 'Bradford's History "of Plimoth Plantation": From the Original Manuscript: With a Report of the Proceedings Incident to the Return of the Manuscript to Massachusetts' [1898] Bradford, William August 10, 2009, Cornell University Library

8. Bradford's History "of Plimoth Plantation": From the Original Manuscript

9. Karen Ordahl Kupperman *Indians and English: Facing Off in Early America* p. 190 (Cornell University Press 2000)

10. The Jamestown Massacre described in - *A History Of The Colonies Planted By The English On The Continent Of North America, From Their Settlement To The Commencement Of That War Which Terminated In Their Independence* Philadelphia, Marshall John p. 58 (A. Small, 1824)

11. "what's done is done" *Macbeth* Act 3, Scene 2

12. Detailed study of the vegetation and ecology prior to the arrival of the Puritans. *Changes in the Land. Indians, Colonists, and the Ecology of New England* Cronon, William (Hill & Wang 1983)

13. John Slany's brother Humphrey imported wine on The Mayflower less than nine months before she sailed to America, so there is every possibility Squanto would have heard of the request for the ship. *Making Haste from Babylon: The Mayflower Pilgrims and Their World: A New History* Bunker, Nick (Pimlico 2011)

14. Carolus Clusius born in Arras, was a pioneering botanist who heard about Drake's voyage and travelled to London to interview Drake and his crew. His cabinet of curiosities in Leiden and the educational garden he designed and laid out there, were famous throughout Europe and William Bradford would have had easy access to it when living there. *The Paradoxal Compass, Drake's Dilemma* Morpurgo, Horatio. p. 130 (Notting Hill Editions 2017)

15. 'Shakespeare's Magical Music Box: The Sound Of Rapture at The Globe' Kampen, Claire van. *The Guardian* 21 Aug. 2016

16. According to Prynne's long essay theatre "corrupt the minds, the manners, the vertuous education...of Gentlemen...by drawing them on to idlenesse, luxury ...and other dangerous vices which plays and Playhouses oft occasion" 'Histrio-Mastix : The players scourge, or, Actors Tragaedie' Prynne, William 1633. Princeton Theological Seminary Library. Godfrey Davies summarises the essay p. 396 The Early Stuarts

17. This is Edward Winslow's description of the incident: As we wandered we came to a tree, where a young sprit was bowed down over a bow, and some acorns strewed underneath. Stephen Hopkins said it had been to catch some deer. So as we were looking at it, William Bradford being in the rear, when he came looked also upon it, and as he went about, it gave a sudden jerk up, and he was immediately caught by the leg. It was a very pretty device, made with a rope of their own making and having a noose as artificially made as any roper in England can make, and as like ours as can be, which we brought away with us. *Mourt's Relation: A Journal of the Pilgrims* at Plymouth, University Microfilm (Ann Arbor, Michigan) facsimile edition of the original 1622 edition.

18. "… for one brief moment Plymouth's Principal Patriarch was at the mercy of an Algonquin mechanism. His normal operations were interrupted, and his perspective was involuntarily changed. The Wampanoags had momentarily given him an opportunity to observe the earth from the air and from this unaccustomed elevation, Bradford could see the juxtaposition of New World ingenuity and Pilgrim naïveté. The Indians had turned his position as counsellor and advisor upside down, moved sky to his feet, and pointed his head to the earth. In metaphorical terms, the writer of 'Of Plimoth Plantation' was directed to a page of American Indian narrative. American Indian culture had now forced itself into his consciousness and literally redirected his mind. Bradford, alone of all the others had been touched by an unseen Indian hand and imprinted" p. 55 Betty Booth's 1998 dissertation on 'American Indian Texts embedded in works of Canonical American Literature'

CHAPTER FIVE
O BRAVE NEW WORLD THAT HAS SUCH PEOPLE IN'T

1. William Bradford *Bradford's History of 'Plimoth Plantation'* (The Project Gutenberg eBook) http://www.gutenberg.org/files/24950/24950-h/24950-h.htm

2. Mary E. Gage *Native American Historical Beliefs and Cultural Concepts Applicable to Stone Structures* (2010) http://www.stonestructures.org/html/historic_links_to_stone_structures.html

3. Kenneth M. Morrison *The Embattled Northeast: The Elusive Ideal of Alliance in Abenaki-Euramerican Relations* p. 66 (University of California Press 1984)

4. Although he writes about his earlier difficulties in Virginia, John Smith then writes about the difference in the much friendlier approach of natives in New England and how much easier it was to trade with them "The Saluages have entreated me to inhavit where I will" *New England's Trials* Smith, Captain John 1620 reprint with prefatory note by Charles Deane (Cambridge Press John Wilson & Son 1873)

5. Colin G. Calloway *Dawnland Encounters: Indians and Europeans in Northern New England* (University Press of New England 1991)

6. "What's gone and what's past help should be past grief." Gigi's family saying from *The Winter's Tale*

7. First Hundred Years: Weymouth, Massachusetts Clarke, Theodore G. "Ted" https://www.weymouth.ma.us/history/pages/first-hundred-years

8. Battlefields of the Pequot War: Pequot Museum and Research Centre Mistick Fort Campaign Connecticut May 26, 1637 http://pequot-war.org/about/

9. "Suddenly, a dog barks. The awakened Pequots shout Owanux! Owanux! (Englishmen! Englishmen!) and mount a valiant defense. But within an hour, the village is burned and 400-700 men, women, and children are killed. Captain John Underhill, one of the English commanders, documents the event in his journal, Newes from America: Down fell men, women, and children. Those that 'scaped us, fell into the hands of the Indians that were in the rear of us. Not above five of them 'scaped out of our hands. Our Indians came to us and greatly admired the manner of Englishmen's fight, but cried "Mach it, mach it!"—that is, "It is naught, it is naught, because it is too furious, and slays too many men." Great and doleful was the bloody sight to the view of young soldiers that never had been in war, to see so many souls lie gasping on the ground, so thick, in some places, that you could hardly pass along. http://www.pequotwar.com/history.html

10. "Sell a Country? Why Not Sell the Air? In 1810, Tecumseh faced Governor William Henry Harrison to bitterly protest the land sales of 1805 – 1806. Below is a section of the statement Tecumseh made to the governor. *"The way, the only way to stop this evil is for the red men to unite in claiming a common and equal right in the land, as it was at first, and should be now—for it was never divided, but belongs to all. No tribe has the right to sell, even to each other, much less to strangers…. Sell a country! Why not sell the air, the great sea, as well as the earth? Did not the Great Spirit make them all for the use of his children?"* Turner III, Frederick ed., The Portable North American Indian Reader (New York: Penguin, 1987), 245 – 46.

11. This is the inscription written in Latin on Bradford's gravestone

CHAPTER SIX
UNLUCKY DEEDS – LIKE THE BASE INDIAN, THREW A PEARL AWAY, RICHER THAN ALL HIS TRIBE

1. *Lives of the Governors of New Plymouth and Massachusetts Bay.* Bailey Moore, Jacob p. 58 (Publishers Gates & Steadman New York 1848)
2. https://en.wikipedia.org/wiki/William_Bradford_(governor)#Family
3. Robert Gorges was the son of Sir Ferdinando Gorges Governor of Plymouth fort in Devon and briefly became Governor-General of New England from 1623 to 1624. *The New England Historical and Genealogical Register*, Vol 26 (Society's House Boston 1872)
4. John Smith claims that he left Captain Thomas Hunt to carry his fish to Spain to market but instead Thomas took 24 natives and sold them into slavery in Malaga Spain. *The Life of Captain John Smith: The Founder of Virginia.* Gilmore Simms, William p339 (Sanborn, Carter, Bazin & Co. Boston 1846)
5. With the help of some friars, Squanto made it back to England and was indentured to John Slany of The Newfoundland Company. *The Red Atlantic: American Indigenes and the Making of the Modern World, 1000-1927* Weaver, Jace p. 59 (UNC Press Books 2014)
6. Thomas Dermer had been an officer under Captain John Smith and remembered Squanto from that voyage. He was then commissioned by Sir Ferdinando Gorges to explore New England with Squanto in 1619. *The History and Future of Narragansett Bay.* Jones, Capers p. 82-3 (Universal-Publishers, Boca Raton, Florida 2006)
7. William Cronon *Changes in the Land, Indians, Colonists and the Ecology of New England* (Hill & Wang NY 1983)
8. https://homeguides.sfgate.com/native-american-method-growing-corn-69787.html
9. Jacka Bakery in the cobbled streets of the Barbican in Plymouth claims to be the oldest commercial bakery in the country and that their ovens supplied biscuits to *The Mayflower* passengers https://www.maturetimes.co.uk/greater-british-bake/

10. Caliban's speech from Shakespeare's *The Tempest* which was used in the opening ceremony of the 2012 Olympics

11. Drake's Leat, was one of the first municipal water supplies in the country it was proposed when Sir Francis Drake was Mayor of Plymouth and then he also sat on the select committee which decided on its funding. Although the main purpose was to supply water for Naval and Merchant shipping Drake also added a clause allowing his family to build windmills to operate along the Leat. *Drake's Leat: Safe Water for a City*. Gardner-Thorpe, Christopher Pearn, John. Amphion Press, 2010

12. Ian Mortimer *The Time Travellers Guide to Elizabethan England* p. 21 (Random House 2012)

13. In 1281, King Edward I of England commissioned the Shropshire Knight, Sir Peter Corbet to kill all wolves by any means he saw fit and in under 10 years it looked as if he had finished them off as very few reports occur after this date. *The Last Wolf: The Hidden Springs of Englishness. How the killing of the last wolf in England changed the course of history*. Winder Robert (Little Brown 2017)

14. A quarter or a third of all families in the country contained servants in Stuart times and most were engaged in working the land. *The World We Have Lost, further explored*. Laslett, Peter (University Press Cambridge 2000)

15. Jeffrey L. Forgeng *Daily Life in Stuart England* (Greenwood Publishing Group, 2007) & *Devon Household Accounts 1627-59: Part I* Gray, Todd (ed.)Published by Devon & Cornwall Record Society, Exeter (1996)

16. Crying The Neck is a harvest festival tradition once common in counties of Devon and Cornwall *British folk customs*, Hole, Christina (Hutchinson 1976)

17. In 1603 Sir Ferdinando returned to Plymouth with his wife Ann and his children John, Robert, Ellen and Honoria but both girls died when young. *Gorges of Plymouth Fort* Preston, Richard Arthur p. 126 (University of Toronto Press 1953)

18. William Parker, an Elizabethan adventurer, sea captain and merchant became Mayor of Plymouth in 1601 and was the most famous resident

of Merchant House and most probably modernised the house using the profits from his privateering ventures against the Spaniards in the Caribbean. Sir Ferdinando commissioned him as a Privateer when he was in charge of the fort to spy on the Spanish and then got him involved in the Plymouth Company for the colonisation of the North American coast, founded under the Charter from King James I in April 1606. Parker was also the likely master of the Mary Rose, the victualling ship of Sir Francis Drake's squadron, in the fleet against the Armada in 1588. https://plymhearts.org/merchants-house/about/

19. Miranda Kaufmann has found records of hundreds of Africans living in England in this period; some were independent, some were servants, but none was a slave and one was a sailor who went halfway around the world with Francis Drake. Ports were the most likely places that they were resident and Plymouth and many Devon Parish church records show a number of black baptisms in this era. *Black Tudors, The Untold Story*. Kaufmann, Miranda (OneWorld 2017)

20. Sir Ferdinando Gorges was befriended by the Lord Chief Justice Sir John Popham when he rescued him during the Essex Rebellion and Sir John never forgot Sir Gorges loyalty. pp. 113/126 *Gorges of Plymouth Fort* Preston, Richard Arthur (University of Toronto Press 1953)

21. John Rashleigh, was an English merchant, MP for Fowey and High Sheriff of Cornwall. His ships formed part of the Plymouth pilchard fleet and he captained his own family's ship the Francis of Fowey during the repulse of the Spanish Armada. He was also an early pioneer of Cod fishing in Newfoundland. 'John Rashleigh of Fowey and the Newfoundland Cod Fishery, 1608-20', Scantlebury, Journal of the Royal Institution of Cornwall VII (1978-81)

22. Sir Richard Hawkins commanded a Queen's ship in the Armada but on a later expedition as a privateer, in 1594 he was captured by the Spanish and held prisoner for 8 years. On his return to England he was knighted and elected Mayor for Plymouth and became Vice-Admiral of Devon and in 1605 he was named in the founding charter of the Spanish Company. *A History of Plymouth Vol 1* Jewitt, Llewellynn Frederick William (W.H. Luke Plymouth 1873)

23. On 5th January 1606 Frances Howard at just 14 was married to Robert

Devereux the third Earl of Essex, who was only 13. It was an arranged marriage for clear political and dynastic purposes. *The Trials of Frances Howard: Fact and Fiction at the Court of King James* Lindley, David (Routledge 1993)

CHAPTER SEVEN
THAT IS SHOULD COME TO THIS?

1. Plymouth Borough records have copies of Letters patent, granted by King James I to Sir Thomas Gates, Sir George Somers, Richard Haklyt, Clerk, Prebendary of Westminster, Edward M Wynfield, esq., Thomas Hannam, esq., Raleigh Gilbert, esq., William Parker and George Popham, gentlemen of the London and Plymouth Companies, for the planting of two colonies on the coast of Virginia and America, to be respectively styled the first colony and second colony. Date: 1606

2. The Earl of Southampton, Henry Wriotheseley, a close friend of Shakespeare and Lord Arundel fitted out the early voyage of Captain George Weymouth in 1605. Henry's name is included in the 1605 panel of the New World Tapestry, and he took a considerable share in promoting the colonial enterprises of the time, and was an active member of the Virginia Company's governing council. In her article 'Indian Dances in "The Tempest"' Kelsey, Rachel M. for The Journal of English and Germanic Philology Vol. 13, No. 1 (Jan., 1914), p. 98 (University of Illinois Press) works on a theory that Shakespeare was across a lot of the material relating to early explorations of New England and that there was almost certainly an "American" influence relating to the play.

3. *The Masque of Hymen* was written by Ben Jonson for the marriage of Robert Devereux, 3rd Earl of Essex, and Lady Frances Howard and performed on the 5th January 1606

4. Description of the production in *Hymenæi: Ben Jonson's Masque of Union* Gordon, D. J. (Journal of the Warburg and Courtauld Institutes Vol. 8 1945), pp. 107-145 The Warburg Institute

5. The Westminster trial of the Gunpowder conspirators was held on Jan. 27ᵗʰ 1606 https://www.tudorsociety.com/27-january-1606-trial-gunpowder-conspirators/

6. Jessie "Little Doe" Fermino, a Mashpee Indian, is working to revive the Wampanoag language. In 1993 she had the same dream three nights in a row, she was being spoken to in words she didn't understand but thought they might be her old tribal language. By 2000 she had earned a master's in linguistics, formulated a Wampanoag grammar, and is now teaching the language to tribal members. *Inspired By A Dream* Feldman, Orna (Spectrum, Massachusetts Institute of Technology Spring 2001) http://spectrum.mit.edu/spring-2001/inspired-by-a-dream/

7. Dr. Tarnya Cooper was Curatorial Director at the National Portrait Gallery until 2017 and is currently Curatorial & Collections Director for the National Trust. Dr Cooper led a major seven year research project *Making Art in Tudor Britain* which uses technical analysis to explore the materials, production, influences and patronage of Tudor and Jacobean portraiture https://www.npg.org.uk/blog/authors/tarnya-cooper

8. The British Museum hosted a Shakespeare in London exhibition in 2012. One of the exhibits was a watercolour painting of "*A Virginian Indian at the Zoological Gardens in St James's Park*" This Indian would have been one of a small number of Native Americans brought to England by explorers, and exhibited as curiosities. In *The Tempest*, Trinculo says that English viewers will give ten doits (or low value coins) 'to see a dead Indian' (2.2.32–33). The painting itself came from a friendship album put together by a man named Michael van Meer, who seems to have lived in Hamburg and travelled to London around 1614–15. The album showcases an extraordinary range of paintings of Jacobean London, giving a unique glimpse of Shakespeare's world, https://www.bl.uk/shakespeare/articles/multiculturalism-in-shakespeares-plays

9. The watercolours of John White are amongst the first paintings of America that an English audience had ever seen. His images of an Algonquin chief was the first representation of any native Americans presented to the royal court https://www.smithsonianmag.com/travel/sketching-the-earliest-views-of-the-new-world-92306407/

10. The exhibition about Henry Stuart ran at the National Gallery from

18 October 2012 - 13 January 2013 https://www.npg.org.uk/what-son/the-lost-prince-the-life-and-death-of-henry-stuart/exhibition.php

11. Little is known about William Larkin. He was the son of an innkeeper named William Larkin and lived in the parish of St Sepulchre. His father was a close neighbour of Robert Peake, the portrait painter to Henry, Prince of Wales, and it may have been Peake who introduced Larkin to painting. https://www.npg.org.uk/collections/search/person/mp07212/william-larkin

12. Shakespeare's best documented London property was just across the waters from the Globe in Blackfriars. A plaque on St. Andrew's Hill records that 'On 10th March 1613 William Shakespeare purchased lodgings in the Blackfriars gatehouse located near this site.' The date is known so precisely because the title deed to the property has survived in the archives. https://londonist.com/london/history/where-in-london-did-shakespeare-live

13. The Essex Rebellion never had a detailed plan it was based on belief that overthrowing Elizabeth's government would be widely supported and all they needed to do was give the public a nudge and an uprising would wash over England. Sir Charles Percy's idea was to use the theatre as a stimulus to get Shakespeare's own company to put on a special production of Richard II showing the deposing and killing of a monarch p. 141 *The Life and Achievements of Sir John Popham, 1531-1607: Leading to the Establishment of the First English Colony in New England* Walthew Rice, Douglas Fairleigh (Dickinson Univ. Press 2005)

14. The George Inn Southwark, boasts a list of literary visitors that include Chaucer, Shakespeare and Dickens, https://www.visitbritain.com/gb/en/4-pubs-shakespeare-actually-drank-you-can-too

CHAPTER EIGHT
HEAT NOT A FURNACE FOR YOUR FOE SO HOT THAT IT DOTH SINGE YOURSELF

1. Epenow was captured by a Captain Harlow and was meant to be sold as a slave in Spain however Harlow found that the Spanish considered

Native American slaves to be "unapt for their uses." So instead, Epenow became a "wonder," a spectacle on constant public display in London. Sir Ferdinando Gorges wrote that when he met him, Epenow "had learned so much English as to bid those that wondered him 'Welcome! Welcome!'"

2. Epenow's display in London said to be inspiration of the "strange indian" mentioned by Shakespeare in *Henry VIII*:[3][4] "What should you do, but knock 'em down by the dozens? Is this Moorfields to muster in? or have we some strange Indian with the great tool come to court, the women so besiege us? Bless me, what a fry of fornication is at door! On my Christian conscience, this one christening will beget a thousand; here will be father, godfather, and all together." It was during a performance of *Henry VIII* at the Globe in 1613, a cannon shot employed for special effects ignited the theatre's thatched roof (and the beams), burning the original Globe building to the ground.

3. From 1606 onwards Shakespeare wrote, *Macbeth, Antony and Cleopatra, Coriolanus, Pericles, Cymbeline, The Winter's Tale, The Tempest, Henry VIII* and *The Two Noble Kinsmen. The Tempest* said to be inspired by voyages to America, was first performed on 1 November 1611 before James I and the English royal court at Whitehall Palace.

4. The Official 2012 Olympic Ceremony Programme notes. After walking onto the Glastonbury Tor, Brunel delivered Caliban's "Be not afeard" speech, reflecting Boyle's introduction to the ceremony in the programme. The shows script writer Frank Cottrell-Boyce described the thoughts behind it on the BBC Radio 4 Today programme, 28 July 2012 "Maybe you shouldn't have been able to interpret it that much, because it was about wonder. The theme of the show was to take things that we're very familiar with, and make them seem again wonderful to us: the things that you know about the industrial revolution and the internet, and say 'Aren't these things astonishing, that we live in the middle of?' and to kind of re-polish the pattern of life. So maybe it's alright that you were a little bit bewildered."

5. Princess Red Wing (1896–1987) was a Narragansett and Wampanoag elder, historian, folklorist, and museum curator. She was an expert on American Indian history and culture, and once addressed the United

Nations. https://www.csmonitor.com/1980/1128/112850.html

6. Of Plymouth Plantation Bradford, William 1620-1647

7. *The Tempest* Act V Scene 1. Another Prospero quote – Sir Ian plays the part of Prospero in the 2012 Paralympic ceremony.

8. The suppressed speech of Wamsutta, Frank B. James, Wampanoag, to have been delivered at Plymouth, Massachusetts, 1970 http://www.uaine.org/suppressed_speech.htm

9. The hour's now come, Prospero, *The Tempest* Act I Scene 2

10. We are such stuff, Prospero, *The Tempest* Act IV Scene 2

11. Those who tell the stories, Native American Indian Proverb

12. Getting attached to "things" was considered a weakness. They were a welcoming and communal people, who shared everything and saw possessions as a weakness. So for Squanto to have kept any of his English possessions would have felt a weakness but his painting was clearly something he didn't feel ready at this point to share with other Indians as they wouldn't understand its history. "It is our belief that the love of possessions is a weakness to be overcome if allowed its way it will in time disturb the spiritual balance of man" One tribe in Canada the Micmac told a Frenchman why they held them in contempt "you never cease fighting and quarrelling amongst yourselves, as for ourselves, we live in peace you are envious of each other and usually disparage each other, you are thieves and liars, you are covetous, without generosity and mercy, as for us if we have a piece of bread we divide it amongst ourselves" European Christianity made the growth of institutional authority the hallmark of colonial social life whereas Indian cultures operated in the opposite direction. The Embattled Northeast: The Elusive Ideal of Alliance in Abenaki-Euramerican Relations Morrison, Kenneth M. (University of California Press 1984)

13. Inheritance of property goes down the female line in Indian Algonquin tribes

14. 'How European Americans and Native Americans View Each Other, 1700-1775' http://nationalhumanitiescenter.org/pds/becomingamer/peoples/text3/indianscolonists.pdf

Lightning Source UK Ltd.
Milton Keynes UK
UKHW020637260321
381031UK00011B/668

9 781649 570888